BROKEN LIES

A HOLLYWOOD ROMANCE PART 1

GINA AZZI

Broken Lies

Copyright © 2020 by Gina Azzi

All rights reserved.

No part of this publication may be reproduced, distributed, or transmitted in any form or by any means, including photocopying, recording, or other electronic or mechanical methods, without the prior written permission of the publisher, except in the case of brief quotations embodied in critical reviews and certain other noncommercial uses permitted by copyright law.

This is a work of fiction. Names, characters, businesses, places, events, locales, and incidents are either the products of the author's imagination or used in a fictitious manner. Any resemblance to actual persons, living or dead, or actual events is purely coincidental.

1
ZOE

Two truths and a lie.

Moments ago, Eli Holt, famous Hollywood heartthrob, walked into Shooters Pub and discarded his winter coat and scarf in a booth.

My best friend and co-worker, Charlie, may pass out from excitement.

Meh. Holt doesn't really do it for me.

Liar.

Eli Holt does it for every legally aged vagina in the universe, and a significant number of penises too.

Holt is larger than life, his presence sucking the oxygen straight from the pub. Not just because he's the sexiest man to ever grace this bar — which he is — but because he's a bona fide celebrity hailing from the same streets of our nondescript Chicago suburb.

Even though I don't follow the celebrity news printed in *Gossip* or care about who's dating who in a circle I don't understand, I'd have to be living under a rock to overlook Holt's rugged good looks and dedication to his craft.

He turns toward me, setting off in the direction of the bar, and tugs some of his merino wool sweater up on his forearms. I nearly drool; hard muscle, corded veins, strong hands... where the hell did my chill disappear to?

Green eyes latch onto mine, amiable yet aloof, both present and not. Still, my heart stutters in my chest as his eyes slowly peruse my face, like he's trying to gauge my reaction to him, maybe wondering if I recognize him. Thick, brown hair, cut close to his scalp on the sides and left longer on top, is perfectly styled. Several days of stubble coat his steel jawline, adding an edginess that speaks to the playboy persona celebrated in the tabloids.

He saunters closer, his bulging biceps and strong back pulling at the merino wool, stretching it. Appreciation causes the corners of my mouth to tick up as I drink in his traps and lats the way an art collector salivates over a Basquiat. This man is a rare commodity, a contemporary Adonis, a perfect specimen of male anatomy.

"Hey, can I get a beer?" Fred, one of the regulars, shakes his empty pint glass.

"Not now, Fred," Charlie answers, never dragging her eyes away from the sex god who approaches the bar, commanding the space around him like a drill sergeant.

Heads swivel in his direction. While a logical part of my brain acknowledges it's because he's famous, the nerves and energy dancing around my stomach also know it's because he looks like every bad decision every woman's been tempted to make. At least once.

Green eyes pierce me to my core, causing Charlie to jab me in the ribs with her index finger. "He's going to talk to you," she whisper-hisses.

He stops in front of me, dropping his elbows to the bar. "Hey. A bucket of Heinekens and three shots of your top tequila." His voice is low and rumbly, tugging on the strings that hold my pelvic floor in place.

Jeez Louise.

A full mouth parts, revealing straight, blindingly white teeth. A nose that's been broken at least once somehow adds more character to his face instead of detracting from his rugged good looks. Full eyebrows, a teeny cleft in his chin, a barely noticeable scar above the right corner of his mouth.

"Hey babe. Did you hear me?" He snaps his fingers and my mouth drops open.

Shocked, amused, and a tiny bit embarrassed, I laugh out, "Did you just snap at me?"

"Just getting your attention."

I roll my eyes. "You have the attention of everyone in here."

He shrugs, a playful gleam ringing his irises. "We can take a selfie if you want, so you can study it later in your bedroom."

This time, laughter shoots from my mouth in surprise. Is this guy for real? "Ah, now you had to go and ruin it."

He frowns, a small dip appearing between his eyebrows. "Ruin what?"

"The fantasy playing out in my head." I joke easily, falling back into my role as bartender: engaging, playful, flippant. Grabbing three shot glasses with my right hand and swinging to pull down a bottle of top-shelf tequila with my left, I line up the glasses as I glance at Holt, "You killed it."

One side of his mouth lifts in amusement, his eyes crinkling. "That was never my intention. Now, I'll have to figure out how to get back in your good graces."

I shake my head. "What's the saying about a first impression? You only get one?"

His smile widens.

"That was your one shot to try to pick me up," I continue, unabashedly enjoying our banter as I grab a shaker. "Chilled?"

He nods, leaning closer. Rolling his lips together as if to contain his laughter, his eyes widen with curiosity that washes over me like approval. Like I really earned his attention. "Sweetheart, you would know if I was picking you up. And there wouldn't be any trying on my part." He pulls out his wallet from the back pocket of his designer distressed jeans and places it on top of the bar.

"Ouch," I grin, pouring his shots, enjoying this banter way more than I should. I mean, what kind of a woman brazenly jokes with a Hollywood actor? *The* Hollywood actor? Even though his words just shot me down, they were playful, and his attention never wavered from my face. In fact, with each passing second, his aloofness gives way to friendliness. "Well, I'm sure the women here can't wait to welcome you home with open arms."

He pulls a black AmEx from his wallet and pauses, his mouth curling into a smirk. "I'm just meeting my brother and friend for drinks. If I was looking for a real homecoming, I wouldn't be here. I'd be downtown at Lush." He tilts his head, his gaze still on mine, as he mentions the lavish nightclub known for its exclusivity and bottle service.

I smirk back, winking at him. "The night's still young, Hollywood. I'll have someone bring over your shots and beers." I grasp his credit card and turn, about to start a tab for his table.

I feel his gaze, electric and searching, settle between my shoulder blades, but I refuse to give him the chance to ruin the flirty exchange we just had. I'd never admit it out loud, but it's the type of memory I'll play over in my mind.

"Holy shit." Charlie bumps her hip against mine once

Holt is gone. "Eli Holt looked like he wanted to reach over the bar and tear your clothes off."

"That's unbelievably dramatic, even for you." I move over to the ice chest to shovel ice into a bucket.

"No, I'm serious. He was into you."

I shake my head and roll my eyes. "He's a Hollywood A-lister, Charlie. Engaging with people is probably one of his job requirements."

"He didn't look over at me like that. And I'm a real fan." She huffs, pointing at herself before brandishing her index finger in my face. "You should go talk to him. Maybe even go home with him. That was one hell of a meet cute."

Cracking up at her forward, not to mention ridiculous, suggestion, I grip bottles of Heineken by their necks and bury them in the ice bucket. "You're officially banned from watching any more romantic comedies on Netflix. Besides, he said if he wanted to go home with a woman tonight, he'd be at Lush."

"Damn." Charlie frowns and then shakes her head, glancing at him seated in his booth. "I don't think he meant it."

"*Charlie.*"

"Look, all I'm saying is that you need to have fun. The past few months have been super scary for you –"

"I'm fine." I cut her off so we don't have to have this conversation again.

"I know you're fine. It was just a cyst. But it really spooked you." Charlie lowers her voice, her touch on my forearm filled with sympathy that I shake off.

"Of course it spooked me, Charlie. With my family history and Dad's vision worsening —" I pause, my hand slipping into the back pocket of my jeans. My fingertips collide with the sharp point of the folded-up paper containing my BRCA gene test results to see if I have the mutation that causes an increased risk of breast and ovarian cancers.

I've been carrying it around for nine days and still haven't worked up the courage to share my results with Dad. Or Charlie.

"I know. I didn't mean it like that. I just meant, what's the harm in having some fun? You're always talking about your business and work as the reasons why you can't seriously date. You always say you just want the casual, no-strings-attached guy."

I raise my eyebrows at her, beseeching her to make her point.

She tips her chin at the booth where Holt sits, scrolling on his phone. "What could be more fun and have fewer strings than him?"

I laugh at the absurdity of her explanation. "I love you for looking out for me. But Eli Holt is, well…" I wave a hand in his general direction, "him. And I'm me. I enjoyed our little banter at the bar, but that's the end of it. Here, deliver these to his table." I solidify my point by pressing the tray of shot glasses in her hands.

She sighs, turning toward Eli's booth, the tray balanced on her palm.

However, as she approaches his table and laughs at whatever he says, a pang of curiosity cuts through my chest.

What's so funny? What are they talking about?

Oh my God, Zo! He's here for a drink. You're a bartender.

Your exchange meant nothing. To him or to you.

Forcing myself to get back to work, I slide a free bourbon toward Fred for his patience and scan the bar for other customers.

2

ELI

"So, Violet sent you, huh?" I grin at Blondie as she appears at the end of the booth, balancing a tray of three shot glasses.

"Violet?"

"The purple streaks in her hair."

Blondie giggles. "Got it. It's nothing personal. Zoe just knows I'm a huge fan." She places the glasses down one by one.

But I've already cut my gaze back to the hot bartender. She leans over the far side of the bar and I take in the swell of her ass, my hands itchy to palm her curves. Her body is fit in a way that speaks to long hours working out and eating well. Her dark hair, streaked with violet, is pulled back into a ponytail, the ends curling from a damp sweat. Her sweetheart face is beautiful, even without makeup. But her eyes, golden-honey, bright and burning, are her most defining feature.

A lesser man would gladly drown in those eyes the way a drunk drowns himself in whiskey. Violet's got that extra something that naturally attracts people to her. Then, she opened her mouth, words tumbled out, and I found myself more intrigued by her banter than her beauty.

She's relaxed and nonchalant, and something about her playful rejection fills me with excitement. It's been too long since I had any type of challenge. Violet is unreadable, flirty and fun but distant in a way that would make fucking around with her just as good as fucking her. I bet there's not a single guy in Shooters who's looked at her and not fantasized about taking her right here on top of the damn bar.

"And she isn't?" I dig for more information, not caring that it makes me look pathetic. Not everyone likes your movies, dickhead. As one of Hollywood's favorite tastes of man-candy, I'm not exactly known for playing deep and contemplative roles.

But that's about to change.

I kick back in the booth, stealing another glance at the bar. Why the hell does her brush-off spur me on? Who cares what hot bartender Zoe thinks?

The blonde giggles again. At least she's a fan. "I swear it's not personal. Zoe's super focused and doesn't read *Gossip* or spend hours on social media. She's too busy working."

"Here?"

Blondie nods. "Here and at a gym in the city. She's a trainer, works with some of the MMA guys, and has her own YouTube channel, That Fit Bitch Life."

MMA guys? I gotta ask Connor about her. I glance at my watch; where the hell are my best friend and brother anyway?

"Cool. Well, thanks for the shots."

"No problem. I'll be right back with your beers," Blondie calls over her shoulder. Moments later, she drops off a bucket of Heinekens. "Holler if you need something."

"Yeah, thanks." I pick up a shot glass and glance back at Zoe, hoping she'll look up, but she's too busy wiping down liquor bottles in between filling pints of beer from the tap. Blondie was right — all it takes is one look at Violet to know she's on her grind.

Good for her. I lift my shot glass, tip it in her direction in a silent cheers, and down it.

My phone buzzes with a call from Natalie but I silence it as Evan's voice rings out.

"I swear, you do more in one day than I do in a week." My brother flicks me behind the ear and slides into the booth across from me. He deposits his winter coat and scarf in the corner of the booth and shrugs out of his suit jacket.

"Fancy." I pull a beer from the bucket of ice at the end of our table and slide it to him. "About time you got here."

"Fuck, man." He taps the neck of his bottle against mine. "Billable hours are a bitch."

"Shoulda become an actor. Can't beat that job security."

Evan grins, taking a swig of his beer. "Only if your name is Eli Holt. How was New York?"

Shaking my head, I lean back in the booth, the tension in my shoulders relaxing a notch now that my brother's here and I've got a beer in my hand. Glancing around Shooters, the familiarity of the place coats me in nostalgia.

Sure, the cracked red vinyl covering the booth seats has been updated with a respectable green, and the burnt-out neon signs no longer decorate the walls, but the smell of beer and peanuts is the exact same.

The back corner where some guys are throwing darts is the first place I ever kissed Natalie Beck.

We were sixteen, drunk, and breathless.

The spot next to the pool tables is where she broke my heart.

The first time.

And the second.

It seems masochistic to come back to a place that holds so many awful memories.

And yet, it feels strangely good, one of those bittersweet aches, to breathe in something dependable after months of being in LA, a place I can't seem to call home even though I live there.

"I signed the contract."

"No fucking way." Evan leans forward over the table and stares at me. "You sure you're going to be okay working for *him*?"

I shrug, scrubbing my hand down the length of my face. "Look, Gray Preston is one of the best directors of his time. He's creative, not afraid to push boundaries, a goddamn visionary. I don't have to like him to work with him; I need to respect him. And I do."

"I know, I know." Evan nods in agreement but his gaze is still hesitant. "It's just that with Natalie—"

"That was a long time ago. Preston was nothing but professional, claiming I'm a perfect fit for the role. What am I supposed to do? Turn down a role that could define my career? Pass up the opportunity to work with a director who is revered in the industry just because he married my ex-girlfriend?" I swallow half the contents of my beer, my rhetorical question hanging between Evan and me as agitation works through my body the way it always does at the mention of Natalie.

"I get it." Evan blows out a large breath. "Plus, if you turned down the role, you'd cause a media frenzy."

"A goddamn shitstorm," I agree, imagining the headlines that would paint me as a lovesick puppy, pining for my high school sweetheart. Snubbing Gray Preston would be petty, not to mention stupid. Besides, I've been over Natalie Beck for a long time, years, even though the wounds she inflicted have barely scabbed over. "It's a phenomenal role. A chance for me to break with the general clichés I've been playing and do something bigger, deeper."

Evan nods, reaching over to slap my shoulder. "I'm proud of you, man. You did it. In four years, you've achieved your dreams."

Shaking my head from his heartfelt congratulations, I blow off his honesty. Evan and I are similar in so many ways but when it comes to voicing our feelings, he's always been able to do so freely while I turn inwards, uncomfortable with all the mushiness. Holding up my hand, I remind him, "I'm not there yet."

"Come on, Eli. Enjoy the moment. After everything you've been through, you deserve something good. This next film, the challenge, the opportunity to work with Preston, it's all positive."

"Yeah." I drain my beer and reach for another. "I just wish I had more time here in Chicago before flying out to the Seychelles. Especially to kick it with Ollie." I reference my only nephew, Evan's son, who may as well be mine for how much I love the little shit.

"He's excited you're coming to his game tomorrow."

"Wouldn't miss it." Ollie is hands-down the best player on his soccer team and I catch as many of his games as my schedule allows. Knowing I won't see him play for the next four months makes tomorrow's game extra important.

"I had to show him where the Seychelles is on the globe. We also looked it up in the Encyclopedia Britannica."

"You still have those?" I frown. "No wonder the kid doesn't know who Kawhi Leonard is. I thought they stopped printing those the year I was born."

Evan flips me off. "Ollie's very excited for you to meet some sea turtles."

"I'll send him a hundred pictures." I slide another beer over to my brother and flag down a server. "Is Connor still coming?"

"Yeah, he's finishing up at the gym. He's got a fight coming up soon."

"Too soon," Connor adds, stepping up to the booth, faint bruises on the side of his face and a nasty cut below his left eye.

"You sure you ready for it?" I joke, standing as much as I can in the booth to pull him into a one-armed hug. Yes, the bromance is real.

"Shoulda seen the other guy," Connor jokes, turning to wave at Violet and Blondie. "We'll take six shots of Patron when you have a second, Zoe."

"Sure thing, Con," Violet answers with a cheery grin that punches me in the gut.

When she smiles, her face brightens like the goddamn sun. She literally glows, spreading her warmth to everyone in her orbit. It sucks me in, radiant and cheerful, and irritates me at the same time. Does she smile like that at everyone?

Connor shoves into the booth next to Evan.

"What's the deal with her?" I flip my chin toward Violet.

"Zoe? She's cool." Connor says slowly, his eyes assessing the reason for my interest in the hot bartender.

Moments later, the vacant space fills up again with Harlow, my assistant. Short, spunky, and the opposite of shy, Harlow Reid shakes her head at the three of us, a genuine smile blooming on her face.

"Gang's all here. It's good to see y'all reunited," she quips, her southern roots wrapping around her words in the softest drawl that has Connor shifting in his seat.

"All good, Low?" I ask.

"Wanna beer?" Evan offers.

"I think so. I just need to talk to you about one thing regarding your trainer for location." She wrings her hands. "And I'll pass on the beer, but thanks."

"Jake's coming," I answer, lifting my beer to my lips.

Harlow shakes her head. "I just got off the phone with him. He has some family emergency and won't be able to join you on location."

Two heads swivel in my direction. I don't miss the soft "shit" mumbled under Evan's breath.

I sigh, dropping my bottle back to the table. "Fuck. Seriously?"

Harlow nods.

"But Jake knows my routine, my schedule. Not to mention, where the hell am I going to find a trainer on short notice who can drop everything to come to the Seychelles for four months?"

An awkward silence settles over the table as Evan and Connor stare at their hands or beer bottles.

"You could ask Zoe," Connor offers, breaking the silence.

"The bartender?" Incredulity drips from my tone, condescending and harsh. "I want to fuck her, not work with her," I admit, throwing my cards on the table.

Harlow flinches, turning around to make sure Violet didn't hear me.

"Jesus, man. Lower your voice." Connor urges, giving me a look. "Zoe's a really good trainer. She's got a decent following on her YouTube channel and —"

"YouTube? Connor, this is the film that's going to define my career to date. And you want me to task a bartender I don't even know with —"

"She's talented, man. Really fucking talented. Trains a few guys at the gym. Can hold her own in the MMA circuit. One of her guys is really up and coming. She blends her workouts, pulling in aspects of MMA and traditional weightlifting with cardio circuits. She's respected around here." His voice is hard, his nostrils flaring with irritation for my dismissiveness. A UFC fighter who co-owns a nearby gym, Connor knows everything about who and what is trending in the fitness circle.

I'm being short-sighted, and everyone around this table knows it.

Next to me, Harlow stiffens, her gaze catching on Connor as the corners of her mouth dip.

Interesting.

"You think she'd just pack up and follow me to an island?"

"I think she'd consider a job offer that would allow her to expand her business." Connor's tone is measured but the look he flicks toward Harlow is filled with acknowledgement.

Harlow clears her throat, a slight blush working up her cheeks.

"Hey, what's going on between you guys?" Evan stage-whispers, his eyes cutting between Connor and Harlow.

"Nothing." Connor shuts it down immediately, his voice low, his expression severe. He chances a glance at Harlow but she looks away, tipping her chin up.

Damn, what the hell did go down?

"You're sure about her, Connor?"

"Yeah, man. She's your best bet on short notice. Plus, she's local," he says, knowing that in this neighborhood, we try to help our own when we can.

I nod once, facing Harlow. "You check her out?" I refrain from calling her out for being awkward around Connor. Girl's been with me for the past four years, since my first year in LA. While she's endured a lot of bullshit being my assistant, she's also become like an annoying little sister to me. So, while I can mess with her, I don't let anyone else. Even my brother and best friend.

"Her YouTube Channel, That Fit Bitch Life, is legit. She's also got an insane Instagram following."

"Who does she train?"

"Three guys at my gym. Plus, she does a weekly self-defense class for women," Connor supplies.

Harlow stares at him, nearly in a trance. He holds her gaze, neither one of them wanting to blink first.

For fuck's sake.

I clear my throat, garnering their attention. Connor downs a shot and slams it back on the table. Wiping the back of his hand across his mouth, split knuckles and all, he downs a second, hissing as the alcohol hits the back of his throat.

"Zoe's not on the Hollywood scene, but I think she'd be a good addition to the team," Harlow adds, her voice strained.

"Whatever," I wave a hand, ready to be done with this conversation. Who the hell cares who trains me as long as I step onto set each day ready to own my role? "Talk to her. And, make sure the offer is fair."

"Of course." Harlow gives me a dirty look as if I offended her.

But the way Connor highlighted that Violet is local bothered me. The truth is, outside of my family and friends — my parents, Evan, Ollie, and Connor — I rarely give back to my neighborhood. I got out of here four years ago and ran head-first into the opportunity that awaited me. Looking back never held the same appeal as moving forward. For these past four years, I've been sprinting like an Olympian. "Anything else, Low?"

"Nope. Have a good night, guys." She turns and unbuckles the belt on her winter coat as she walks up to the bar, stopping in front of Zoe.

My chest tightens and I clench my shot glass. Ripping my gaze from the interaction unfolding between Harlow and Zoe, I distract myself by turning toward Connor, ready to rake him over the coals for crushing like a prepubescent boy on Harlow. "What the hell is up with you and Low?"

He shakes his head, his expression hard, his eyes darkening to black.

Blowing out a breath, I tilt my head to the bar. "She's staying for drinks."

"I'll make sure she gets home okay."

I raise my eyebrows.

Connor stares back, his face blank, his eyes burning. "Not like that, just that she gets home okay. On her own," he adds, causing Evan to chuckle. "What time is Ollie's game tomorrow?" Connor ignores the suspicious and skeptical glances he's getting and directs his question toward my brother.

Taking a swig of my beer, I let him change the subject, knowing now isn't the right time to get into whatever is going on between my friend and my assistant behind closed doors.

Now, more than ever, I need to focus on my career, on my role in *Dangerous Devils*.

My gaze flits back to Zoe. She's a distraction I don't need even though I'm stuck with her. Zoe the hot bartender/YouTuber better know what the hell she's doing. Even though I'm drawn to her, body and mind, her flirty quips and amused grins aren't going to cut it in the Seychelles if she doesn't show up to work.

3
ZOE

"You're Zoe Clark." The petite girl with a thin hoop in her nose unwraps her winter coat and slips onto a barstool.

"Who's asking?" I glance over at Eli Holt, fan favorite for playful heartbreaker, suspecting he's somehow involved.

"Me."

Grinning, I cock my head toward the table of stupidly good-looking men. I know Connor. Since he's good people, I decide to cut this girl some slack. "You work for Hollywood?"

"I'm Harlow Reid. Eli's assistant."

I place a bar napkin in front of Harlow. "What are you drinking?"

"Jack and Coke." She twists on her bar stool, shooting the leery man next to her a dirty look which causes me to smile. I like her unabashed honesty. "Listen, Eli "

"I'm not interested in sleeping with Eli Holt. I think he's hot, but I'm not one of those groupie fans." I add extra Jack to her drink because being at anyone's beck and call can't be easy. Plus, the furtive glances she and Connor keep exchanging are giving me anxiety, so I can only imagine it's more stressful for her.

At my words, she shakes with silent laughter, her eyes gleaming with amusement. "That's good, because I'm not here to proposition you on his behalf."

I facepalm, silently swearing at Charlie for putting these stupid thoughts in my head. "That's a relief. It's just, this place, it's a neighborhood pub. We don't cater to the rich and famous. We don't even cater to the deep pockets and smooth talkers. It seems Hollywood may be more comfortable at a downtown club."

Harlow takes a gulp of her drink, snorting laughter at my words. "Trust me, Eli likes it here just fine."

"Okay." I fill my water glass with ice. "Can I get you anything else?"

"Yes." She shifts closer, dropping her voice. "I've been following you on That Fit Bitch Life for months."

"Seriously?" I pause, a flicker of pride swelling in my chest.

Harlow takes a sip of her Jack and Coke. Placing the glass back down on the bar, she stares directly at me. "Eli wants to offer you a job."

I take a step back, my momentary pride flaring into confusion. Why would Hollywood offer me a job? Because he thinks he wounded me with his brush-off? I've got thicker skin than that. I've got thicker skin than most people I know. It comes with the territory of spending hours on this side of the bar. I've perfected flirty without flirting, listening without judging, and tossing out quips even when my insides are exploding with anger. "Jeez Louise. Harlow, I'm sure you're a nice girl, but Hollywood doesn't even know me. He doesn't have to take pity on —"

"It's not like that. Real talk, he's scheduled to fly to location on Monday to film *Dangerous Devils*."

"The Gray Preston movie?"

"Exactly. His regular trainer can't leave L.A. at the moment, and Eli needs a trainer on short notice. Connor…" She shoots a reticent glance at the UFC fighter downing shots in the corner. Well, at least the attraction, or lack thereof, is mutual, "Connor vouched for you."

"He did?" My heart rate ticks up, cantering in my chest. I squeeze the ledge of the bar. This could be an opportunity, an in, a chance to take my business to the next level. While I'm not exactly strapped for cash, Shooters is. This pub is Dad's financial future. Between his worsening blindness and my uncertain medical issues, I can't afford to pass up on any opportunities that allow me to save money. But, "There has to be a million more qualified people."

"There are."

"So?" I raise an eyebrow, my silent question hanging in the air between us: why did he pick me?

"He needs someone out of the L.A. circle. Someone good at their job who is going to put the training, the film, first. Who isn't going to get caught up in the limelight and the moment."

"And you think that person is me?"

"I do." Harlow nods seriously, dragging the bottom of her glass across the bar. "I know you don't know me and have no reason to trust me, but I was prepared to send you an email and offer you a job. I had no idea you worked here until Connor pointed you out."

Grabbing a pint glass, I fill up a draft of Bud for Fred before stepping back in front of Harlow. "Look, I have a job and —"

"$200K."

"What?"

"Come to location, train Eli for the next four months. The salary is $200,000."

My body nearly drops, my legs turning to literal jelly underneath me. I grip the bar to keep from falling. "You're joking."

"I'm not. This is a once-in-a-lifetime opportunity, Zoe. Not because of the scope of work, but because of the buzz surrounding this film, surrounding Eli. That, plus the salary will funnel directly into your business. You could level up in a quarter of the time it will take you if you stay here and turn this job down."

Her words are the answers to the frantic questions I've been spinning around in my mind for the past nine days.

How am I going to insure Dad's future financial stability if Shooters goes under?

How am I going to maintain the quality of his medical coverage as his vision worsens?

And, more difficult to consider, what if I die the way Mom and Grandma did? Who's going to care for Dad then? When he no longer sees the shadows and the flickers of light. When his white cane is permanently attached to his hand.

How will he carry on when there's no one here to support him?

Two hundred thousand dollars for four months of work.

Harlow's wrong. This opportunity won't allow me to level up in a quarter of the amount of time it would take if I stay in Chicago. This opportunity grants me the type of financial freedom I crave much faster than that.

And right now, with my BRCA results burning though my pocket, the bottom line of Shooters worsening with each passing month, and Dad's next set of eye exams on the horizon, time is not on my side. "You're serious?"

"I'll send over the contract within the hour."

"I'll look at it."

"Good. If it's satisfactory and you sign, you'll be flying out next week."

"To where?"

"Details will only be provided after you sign an NDA."

"Health insurance."

"What?" Harlow pauses, her drink halfway to her mouth.

"I need health coverage."

She squints at me, as if she can't understand why, after offering me two hundred thousand fucking dollars for four measly months of work, I'd ask for something so ridiculous. Obviously, I could just buy it.

But I need the no-strings-attached kind of insurance that Hollywood could offer.

"It's full. Dental and vision included. For a year."

"Great. I'll wait for the contract." I say the words breezily but inside, I nearly implode. Full medical coverage.

The paper in my back pocket blinks in my mind, like a neon sign I can't fully turn off.

Harlow nods, slipping off the barstool and shrugging into her coat. "What do I owe you?"

I roll my eyes and offer her a genuine smile. "Get out of here, Harlow Reid. I think you just changed my life."

"Not me, Zoe. It's really all him." She points to the booth where Eli and his friends are sitting just as he looks up. His eyes, those hypnotizing pools of green, slam into me. "Hope to hear from you." Harlow slips away as Eli and Connor stand from the booth.

Connor beelines for the door as Harlow slips outside, tying her coat around her tiny waist.

Hollywood stalks toward me, like a predator to his favorite prey. His steps are measured, his eyes cool, assessing. The playful gleam from earlier is gone, replaced with a severity I don't understand. Nearly every head in the place swivels again as he passes.

He towers above the other patrons, easily over 6"3', and his build... I gulp.

His build is the stature of most men's aspirations.

I would know. I train mostly men.

His coiled muscles have sprung open, his incredible eyes bore directly into mine, and his expression is a heady mixture of desire and need laced with a ribbon of uncertainty.

Damn.

I falter back half a step from being the sole focus of so much intensity.

"You're really a trainer." He stops before me, dropping his elbows onto the bar and hunching closer.

A pregnant pause hovers between us. The energy shifts now that I know I'm going to see him again. A lot. This isn't just a random exchange at a bar. We're going to be working together. The playful quips from earlier dissolve on my tongue as I stare at him, unsure of what to say.

My hands grow clammy, my mind foggy.

His face, those eyes, the way his presence eats up all the air slams into me with the force of a linebacker.

He stares back, unbridled curiosity coloring his eyes as he opens his mouth and words pour out.

I blink, straining to catch his words.

Deafening silence clogs my ears, and then the noise and chatter of the pub explodes in my head. I return to the moment as if I've come up from underwater for oxygen.

Pulling air into my lungs, I stare into his hypnotizing face and lose the ability to speak.

"Didn't take you for a fan." A wry smile twists his mouth, his lips almost too full to be masculine. His eyes drink me in before his expression falls and he wraps a hand around my wrist. "Hey, you okay?"

It's at that moment, when my thoughts are a muddled mess of excitement and hope and fear, the moment where he freely gives me empathy, that I regain my composure.

Kind of.

"Your assistant just offered me a job."

His grin widens, his hand tugging me closer until my ribs collide with the edge of the bar.

I hope none of my customers need anything right now, because I'm completely useless. The only person I can focus on is Eli Holt.

Hollywood.

And the incredible shade of his eyes.

The hard line of his jaw.

The shadow of stubble grazing the planes of his face.

Jeez Louise.

"You ready for this, Zoe?" He breathes it out, the sound of my name on his lips doing things, delicious things, to my insides.

And in this moment, I know, just *know* everything is about to change.

I'm going to take this job offer.

I'm going to fly to wherever Hollywood is filming.

And I'm going to lose a piece of myself to Eli Holt.

4

ELI

"You ready for this, Zoe?" I ask, my thumb swiping across the soft skin on the underside of her wrist. She shivers at my touch and I move my thumb again, fascinated by her body's response to me.

How is this girl, the sexy bartender mixing drinks, the chick who laughs at fake insults and flirts with abandon, also the badass trainer Harlow advocated for and Connor stamped with his approval?

She stares down at where I'm touching her but I don't drop my hold. Instead, I press my thumb until it causes an indent in her skin and she glances back up.

"I'm not sure yet."

"Not sure about what?"

"If I'll take the job," she lies, her eyes flickering with mischief.

Laughter clogs my throat, filling the space between us. "Why wouldn't you take the job?"

"Isn't it bad business to accept an offer without reading it first?"

I nod in agreement. "Fair enough."

"Plus, the fine print." She bites her bottom lip.

My eyes zero in on the movement and I narrow my gaze. Is she toying with me? Playing some kind of game?

"Is there any fine print I should know about, Hollywood?" she presses.

I shake my head, dropping her wrist. "No. It's a purely professional relationship." I hate that I'm cock-blocking myself, but it's the right thing to do. Messing around with employees complicates everything, the film included. I won't do anything to jeopardize my performance as Dr. Henry Shorn.

At my words, something I can't place flashes in Zoe's eyes but then she blinks and relief floods her gaze. "Good." She smiles, a dimple popping in her left cheek. It's so her, I realize, to have some of that bubble-gum innocence contrasting with her purple streaks and quick mouth. She's a goddamn enigma. Too friendly to be flirting, too dismissive to be looking for a hook-up. She's too damn confusing to figure out one way or the other. And that's what piques my interest, has me studying her like an equation that's going to end climate change. "Because if I take the job, I'm doing it for real."

"I'd hope so."

"That means you show up, every day, every session, ready to work."

"I will."

"You can ask around about me. The guys I train, they're on time, they work hard, and they check whatever is going on in their personal lives at the door."

While a part of me is impressed by her professionalism, the unwarranted accusation in her tone pisses me off. I step back for a moment, cracking my neck. Violet looks at me, her eyebrow quirking in challenge.

Screw this.

Leaning back over the bar, I crowd her until I can grasp her wrist again. Placing her hand against my abdomen, I cover it with mine. "I'm all muscle, babe. Worked real fucking hard for this body. And my career. You think I just got it based off my good looks and winning personality?"

"Winning personality is a stretch." She chuckles, and the sound turns me on as much as it pisses me off. Add that to my commitment to keep things professional, and I suddenly feel off kilter. Violet is somehow in the driver's seat, taking control, while I flub around unsure of what to do or say next.

Dropping her hand, I step back. "I do the work, Violet. And I expect the same from my team."

She regards me curiously, some of the laughter fading from her expression. "My program, my routine, you're really in?" she questions quietly, ignoring my nickname for her.

I nod once, a curt snap of my neck. "I just need to maintain my current build. Can't bulk up or lean out for the character I'm playing. It's all in the contract. You need to accept all the terms outlined and be okay with them for us to work together."

She pauses for a moment before acceptance slips into the melted butter of her eyes, and she nods. "Okay. I'll take a look at everything. If it's all as Harlow explained, I'll see you on location, Hollywood." She starts to turn away.

"Wait a minute." I reach out again.

Jesus, this is becoming a habit.

And not one I particularly like.

I feel like I'm chasing this woman with absolutely no end goal in mind.

She's about to become one of my employees. A member of my team.

With the exception of Harlow, who's stuck with me from

the start, and my publicist Helen, who demands I interact with her, I don't really give a shit about most of the people I'm forced to associate with in my professional space. The expectation is that everyone shows up to work. Beyond that, I don't care what people do or don't do.

Zoe pauses, gazing at me over her shoulder.

The space between us crackles to life, alive with an energy that wraps around me, drawing me closer to Zoe. She's dangerous, with her heartfelt eyes and perfect curves, accentuated by her obvious training. The tilt of her jaw confident, the flicker in her eyes all unwanted vulnerability.

But damn if she doesn't fill the inside of my mouth with curiosity. Doesn't intrude on my thoughts with layers of questions.

Blowing out a deep breath, I close my eyes.

So much for no drama.

Shit's about to go off the rails.

I can feel it in the invisible thread urging me closer to Zoe, sense it in the way I give the slightest shit that I can't put my finger on what makes her tick.

This girl's going to make me yearn for the heartbreak of Natalie Beck.

Force me to recall the series of shallow hook-ups since Natalie with a fondness.

I can already tell Zoe's got a backbone of steel, a heart of gold, and a body like a goddamn temple.

For the first time since Natalie blew up my world four-and-a-half years ago, I feel my body stir to life. My dick starts to harden for something more than just a willing body and a firm set of tits. Sure, Zoe's slamming, all lean muscle and delicious curves I'd like to sink my teeth into, but it's not that. Girls have gotten me off on less.

It's the brazen way she meets my gaze, the confidence

that oozes from her pores in place of perfume, the ridiculous and unexpected things that drop from her mouth like breadcrumbs, leading me closer to *her*.

"How badly do you need the money?"

"Excuse me?" she falters, tugging on her wrist. Her eyes widen, a blaze of panic ringing her irises.

I tighten my hold. "I'm not asking to be a dick. I'm asking because the job isn't easy. It's long hours, a lot of bullshit, cattiness. And I've been told working with me isn't exactly a picnic."

"Nothing worth achieving is ever as simple as a picnic." Her tone is subdued, in contrast to the bubbly chuckle from earlier. It's threaded with a crestfallen wisdom someone her age shouldn't possess. It pisses me off that she has it.

"Is the money worth your sanity?" I smirk, wanting to push her to the edge. Of what? I don't know but I want her to snap. It will make it easier between us if I know how to get to her. If I understand at least something about her.

She looks up at me and squares her shoulders. Yep, hot girl's tough as nails. She'll make for a good trainer. And a fucking headache all rolled into one.

"Right now, it's worth everything," she shoots back as I squeeze her delicate wrist.

Her words are a disappointment. I don't know why, as they're the words I wanted her to say.

"Then say yes." I hold her gaze. "Take the job."

"I am." A blush works up the column of her neck, spreading into her cheeks. "Your name holds too much weight to turn down. And the salary is too good to pass up."

"Pack your bags, babe. I'll see you in the Seychelles soon."

Her eyes widen, a shimmer of excitement breaking through the confusion swirling in their honey depths.

That's right, baby. I can give you the fucking world.

The five-star hotels.

The private jets.

The all-access pass to every designer, stylist, and restaurant you desire.

And fill you up with so much emptiness, you'll ache to feel whole.

"You better show up to do the work, Hollywood," she taunts, but her teasing tone doesn't match the ferocity in her eyes.

"I'm gonna give you everything, babe. Every. Damn. Thing."

She signed the contract.

Not that I thought she wouldn't, but part of me hoped she'd be smarter.

Or that she would do me a solid and make things easier for me. Working with her is going to test my commitment to not screw a woman on my team.

"Your boarding pass is already in the wallet on your phone. I've forwarded your hotel confirmation and the numbers of anyone who may assist you with any issues. You're in the hotel's penthouse, full ocean view. You have one day to get over the jet lag and then you're jumping into production. Hair and makeup will be on set. I'm still arranging for your trailer or private space. But don't worry, I'll have it all sorted by Wednesday." Harlow grins, passing me a thin envelope, no doubt stuffed with two neatly typed pages of everything I could possibly need for any wish or whim that may arise.

Chances are, I won't even open it.

"Got it." I pick up my coffee mug and take a large gulp. Sleeping on Evan's futon is no joke, but it allows me extra time with Ollie so, I endure. "Want caffeine?"

"Nope. I've already guzzled three iced coffees and feel kind of wired. Like I can't stop smiling."

"Your face looks like it's about to crack."

"Any other questions?"

"You're flying down with the new girl?"

"Zoe? Yes."

"You think she'll get along with everyone okay?"

Harlow gives me a look. "Um, have you met her? I feel like she's the only person on your team who can get along with everyone."

"Why do you say that?" I ask, leaning my hip against the kitchen island.

"She doesn't have an ego and I think she cares more about the work than the celebrity sightings. With her work ethic, she'll probably even impress Preston."

I falter at the mention of his name. "Why would she even meet him?" I try to sound casual but my tone is too alarmed to pull it off. Gray Preston is one hell of a director. I admire his work a lot more than I'd like to admit, and I hate that I'm in an inferior position by accepting this role to work under him.

Before he was Natalie's ex, he was her husband. Her successful, good-looking, well-connected husband. *That* pisses me off at the cellular level because his presence in Natalie's life was as welcome as a cheetah to a kid's fourth birthday party.

But then he up and left her, and I realized that when you care for someone the way I once cared for Natalie, even her failed relationship didn't bring the satisfaction I was searching for.

Still, he won't get his hands on Violet.

Why would he, though? Their roles won't ever overlap.

"I meant it as an example." Harlow rolls her eyes, missing the fact that her off-the-cuff remark sent my mind into overdrive. "Gray's known for running a tight ship. Someone with Zoe's commitment and dedication to her role would probably impress even him."

"Yeah. True." I swallow down the bolt of anger that rose to the surface at the thought of Gray and Violet.

Jesus, I've got to get over my infatuation with this girl. We're going to be working together, and I need to dedicate everything I am to this film.

"You all good?" Harlow asks, her eyes darting to the door.

I wave a hand, indicating that she's free to leave. "Yeah. I'll see you in the Seychelles."

"Don't forget your sunscreen," she says cheerily, practically bouncing out the front door.

"Maybe skip your next iced latte," I call after her.

"No kidding," she sings back, the door closing behind her.

Moments later, the greatest, most important person in my life comes zooming around the corner and jumps on me. Catching Ollie easily, I grin at the little shit. "What's up, little man?"

"You're really here!" He hugs me tighter, his small face burrowing into my shoulder.

I used to hate kids. Not saying it to be a dick, just honest. It's not because of anything they ever did, I just didn't give a shit about other people's snot-nosed little monsters.

When Evan called me that Sophie gave birth, however, I walked off set and went straight to the airport. Hearing the overwhelming happiness in my brother's voice was enough to make me want to see what the big deal was.

And Ollie, he is a big fucking deal.

The first time I held his wrinkly, splotchy little body and breathed in his bald head, a protectiveness I never thought possible hijacked my emotions. I love him fiercely.

Even more so after his crappy excuse for a mother hightailed it out of town in search of her next fix a year ago.

My protective streak toward Ollie increased again when several of the starved supermodels I dated tried to fabricate pregnancy scares, wanting me to believe that I could have my own perfect little boy.

If only they knew it's my greatest wish, just with a woman worthy of being my baby's mother.

But this smelly, silly, perfectly smiley six-year-old somehow makes all the bullshit, all the deceitful lies and elaborate fabrications of the women I keep tangling with, bearable.

"I promised you, didn't I?"

"Yeah, but you also promised me a helicopter ride for my birthday."

Snorting, I nod. "Truth, little man. Take that one up with your dad."

"Hey, don't go taking sides. We need a united front." Evan scolds me as he enters the kitchen, buttoning up the rest of his shirt.

I turn my attention back to Ollie. "Ice cream after soccer?"

"Even if we lose?"

"You're not going to lose. You're going to —"

"Have a great time with your friends," Evan cuts me off, shooting me a look.

"Don't even tell me they get participation trophies," I

mutter. That's why kids today are so unlikable. They're whiny, used to always getting their way. When Evan and I were kids, you either won or you lost. There was no such thing as "participating."

Ollie smiles, hooking his legs around my waist. "Nah, just ribbons."

"That's even worse," I groan. "You let him play in these bogus —"

"All the leagues are like that today," Evan interrupts me.

"Not the ones at the top," I shoot back.

"So, ice cream?" Ollie refocuses me on the priority at hand.

"Ice cream, no matter what," I agree before tossing him over my shoulder like a sack of potatoes. "Now surrender to your master!" I run through the living room, dropping Ollie onto his bed. "The tickle master." I go in, tickling the hell out of my favorite, and only, nephew.

He laughs and squirms, nearly kicking me in the face. Dodging his swinging arms and frantic legs, I pull him into a tight hug as our laughter settles down. "Gonna miss you, kid."

"Me too, Uncle Eli. Don't forget to bring me back a sea turtle."

5

ZOE

"Hey Jetsetter. Can you believe you're going to fly business class? Living the life of the rich and famous!" Charlie kisses my cheek before pushing past me into my studio. "Please tell me you packed that fantastically slutty lingerie I made you buy last Valentine's Day."

I blush at her words and Charlie cheers. "Thank God, soul sister. It's about to be off-trend, so please try to wear it at least once."

"Okay," I hold up a hand. "First off, I did wear it."

"With who?"

"That guy from Colombia who was visiting his sister over the summer."

"Nice." Charlie grins, clearly impressed.

"Secondly, stop talking about sex, even indirectly. My dad's going to be here any minute."

"Helping friends get laid is the whole point of friendship," Charlie adds under her breath, taking a look around my apartment. "I can't believe I'm not going to be here for four whole months, but I'm glad you were able to sublet." A ribbon of sorrow rounds out her words and I wince.

"I can't believe I'm not going to see *you* for four months."

"We'll FaceTime every day," my bestie assures me.

I swallow, my throat dry, my anxiety over what I'm about to do heightening the closer the clock ticks to my departure time. "What the hell am I thinking, Charlie? Who agrees to a job where you have to move in one week and have no idea what to expect?"

"I would. In a heartbeat. Especially if the man offering the job was Eli freaking Holt!" She yells the last part, whooping loudly and pumping her fist like a bad character from *Jersey Shore*.

I wrinkle my nose at my best friend, my rock, the one person to keep me grounded when everything feels like it's spiraling out of control. "I'm going to the Seychelles. For four months. Alone."

"I have no idea why you're saying it like it's a bad thing." Charlie clucks her tongue. "I'd donate a kidney to go anywhere for four months."

"But my dad and the bar —"

"Everything will be fine without you. No offense. I know you're integral to Papa Clark's life, and you think no one else can deal with Sunday Night Football at Shooters like you, but babe, everyone and everything are going to be fine."

I scowl. "He has a bunch of appointments coming up —"

"Send me the dates and I'll remind him. I'll even drive him, swear it, if no one else is available."

"I know. It's just, his vision is getting worse. What if —" I bite my lip, not able to keep the quiver out of my voice.

"He won't." Charlie wraps me in a hug, squeezing tightly.

"How do you know? In four months, he could be completely blind."

"He'll always see you, Zoe. You're his North Star. You

need this, babe. It's a good opportunity for you, professionally and personally. All you've done since your grandma passed —"

I step out of her embrace and shake my head, cutting her off as my eyes burn with unshed tears.

"You can't stop living your life, Zoe. This is a once-in-a-lifetime opportunity. Your business is taking off. Imagine what working with a client like Holt will do for your brand? You can grow That Fit Bitch Life by filming workouts and video clips on the beach in the *Seychelles*. Don't you think your viewers would prefer that backdrop more than your bedroom or a dingy gym in Chicago?"

I snort, nodding at her point.

"Besides, the money's fucking awesome. It will take care of some of the financial stress you have about Shooters. You deserve this time to get away, have fun, be a normal twenty-four-year-old obsessed with being tan and having a great holiday romance story. And if that romance just happens to be Eli Holt, you'll make me the proudest friend ever. If not, I'll still tolerate you."

I laugh, emotion crawling up my throat at her words, at the meaning behind them. Charlie's been by my side since the beginning. Since before my mom was diagnosed with breast cancer and stolen from our lives when I was thirteen. From before grandma passed two years ago from ovarian cancer. She was there when I got a mozzarella stick stuck in my braces and nearly choked to death after our basketball team won playoffs in middle school. She stood beside my mailbox the afternoon I received my acceptance letter to college. And she showed up at my door with a box of doughnuts from Doughnut Vault the day after I lost my virginity to my first real boyfriend at nineteen.

It's hard to imagine navigating this next chapter, one that

fills me with excitement and nerves and a new set of challenges, without her. I swipe the backs of my knuckles over my eyes, hoping to knock some wayward tears away.

"Aw, Zoe." She pulls me into another hug and I cling to her.

I should tell her about my BRCA results before I leave.

Hell, I should tell Dad.

"You're going to be fine, Zo. I'm going to miss you like crazy, but you deserve this wild adventure. Let yourself embrace it."

Her words are a salve to my scattered nerves. I bite my tongue before my alarming results slip through my lips and ruin the moment.

Instead, I mentally run through my list of motivators for taking this job: financial flexibility, support for Dad's future, catapulting my business to the next level, having some much-needed fun after years of grief and fear.

Charlie's right; I *need* to go.

"Have you heard from him at all?" She steps back, placing her hands on my shoulders.

"Eli? No, just his assistant, Harlow. And his agent. Both are friendly and professional. They walked me through my job responsibilities and sent over a bunch of paperwork. Helped me get my visa in order and explained accommodations to me."

"So basically, you're all set."

"Basically."

"But no word from Eli. Strange." Charlie shakes her head. "I could have sworn he was into you and that's why he offered you the job."

"Charlie!" I step out of her reach and stick out my tongue. "I am a respectable trainer. Fine, I'm small time and local, but I have great references and am building a solid network. I work with a bunch of well-known guys in the MMA circuit. Rodriguez is about ready to level up. Did you ever consider that Holt offered me this job because he knows I can do it and not just because he thinks I'm a piece of ass?"

"Honestly? No."

Vibrating with a wave of frustration, it crests and breaks with one look at Charlie's unfazed expression. Dissolving into laughter, I lean over, gripping my stomach, tears pricking the backs of my eyelids.

Jeez Louise, I'm a mess.

"Gonna miss that sound." Dad announces his arrival, pushing into my studio apartment with the key he's had since the day I moved out of his home and into my own. He leans his white cane against the molding of my front door and holds out his arms.

"Hi Dad." I walk into his embrace, still giggling/hic-coughing/oh my god, are those more tears? — and wrap my arms around his growing midsection. He grins down at me, his blue eyes pale and cloudy, lines of exhaustion clinging to his features. My dad has worked sixteen- to eighteen-hour days his entire life; he doesn't know the meaning of vacation or the definition of a mental health day.

He's given me everything I ever needed.

Even during his transition into life with physical limitations.

Even as his blindness worsened.

Even when I was lost in the grief of Mom's and then Grandma's deaths.

And now, especially now, it's time I return the favor. Grinning up at him, I squeeze him closer, my resolve for my new job strengthening.

"Hey Papa Clark. Get ready for the best Zoe replacement

you could hope for." Charlie embraces my dad on the other side, earning an affectionate eye roll from him.

"Charlie, promise me you'll come hang at Shooters on Sunday, even if this one is too busy working on her tan." Dad grips Charlie's shoulder.

"I'll do you one even better. I'm picking up Zoe's Sunday shift. I'll be there with my random football jersey on." Charlie grins, her lack of interest in football one of dad's greatest heartbreaks, second only to my preference for basketball.

"Don't doubt that," Dad says, glancing around my apartment. "All set, Zo?"

"All set." I spin to take in my tiny apartment one last time. I don't know why, but the moment seems important.

Deep down, it's as if I know I'm on the precipice of something, and when I return in four short months, everything will be different.

Or at least seem different.

Maybe it will just be me.

"Let's get you to a hot and fabulous island while we all freeze our asses off here," Charlie snickers, gripping the handle of my suitcase and pulling car keys from her pocket.

"Thanks again for driving us." Dad grips his white cane.

"Duh, as if I wouldn't be part of Zoe's send-off committee." Charlie pulls open the door.

"I'm ready." I tug on a hoodie, leaving my winter coat on the coat rack. I definitely won't need it where I'm going. Closing the door behind me, I lock up, and toss Charlie my keys. The guy subletting my place is going to pick them up from Shooters.

Following my dad and Charlie out of the place I've called home for the past four years, I square my shoulders and look to my future.

"OH MY GOD. I feel like I'm in *Lost*." I marvel as the plane begins to descend over Mahe, Seychelles.

"It's beautiful, isn't it?" Harlow leans into me as she cranes her neck to peer out the window. "That's Morne Seychellois, the highest point on Mahe. There are about 115 islands in total but we'll mostly be here, with a few excursions."

"This is incredible." I murmur, my eyes trained to the tall mountain, the wispy clouds wrapping around its peak like a hug, the vibrant blue sky and rolling waves below. "I wish I could parachute into it."

"I'm not sure that's an option, but we can look into skydiving," Harlow says, her voice neutral.

"You must get asked to look into a ton of outrageous things in your line of work."

She cuts me a look, a smirk playing over her mouth. "Zoe, you have no idea."

During our long flight, we had ample time to chat and get to know one another. The more we talked, the more my anxiety faded. Well, I'm sure the champagne helped too, but I like Harlow. I like her unwavering honesty, her direct way of communicating, and her incredible multitasking skills. She's sincere and authentic, and strong women are my spirit sisters.

"Tell me more about what I can expect on a daily basis." I lean back in my seat, gripping the stem of my champagne glass. Just a basic business class bitch here.

"Eli will receive his call sheet the night before. From there, we'll know what time he needs to be in hair and makeup, what scenes he's shooting, etcetera. So your workout times, while he will want to keep them consistent as much as possible, may vary from day to day."

"That's no problem."

"Good. He needs to maintain his current build and potentially add more muscle, but nothing too crazy as it should all look consistent throughout filming."

"Got it. I have a series of circuit trainings I'm going to run him through. In the beginning, it will mostly be to assess his fitness level and flag areas to improve. I understand he wants to perform some of his own stunts?"

Harlow nods.

"Right. So we want to make sure he's ready for them, whatever the nature of the stunt is."

"Yeah. His character is in a plane crash so I imagine it could get pretty wild."

I glance out the window again. What would it be like to be an actor? To routinely slip into someone else's skin and get to be them for a little while? Does it become easier? Are there some skins, some lives, actors ever wish were real?

"Connor backed you really hard," Harlow says unexpectedly. Her tone is too breezy and I hear the unasked question lingering in her voice.

I shoot her a grin. "That was really solid of him. I train three guys at his gym. One of them, Rodriguez, is ready to level up. In a way, my leaving is perfect timing. Rodriguez is thrilled that Connor is going to step in and start training him."

Harlow's face remains blank, her expression carefully neutral.

I shake my almost empty champagne flute at her. "Look, I know I don't really know you, but we just spent something like twenty-two hours sitting next to each other. Plus, champagne. I get the feeling something's up between you and Connor."

Harlow's lips thin as her eyes flash with hurt, which I hate because it indicates that Connor may have been the one to hurt her.

Sighing, I reach out and pat her hand. "Nothing ever happened between Connor and me. Ever. We have a good professional relationship. I consider him an acquaintance. At most, a friend. I've never seen him bring girls around the gym or talk up the fan girls. He's committed to his work, one hundred percent dedicated, and he's an animal in the ring. Outside of the gym, when our paths have crossed, he's always seemed quiet, a bit introverted, but fair. Kind. That's all I got for you."

Harlow's breathing shallows as she absorbs my words.

"You okay?" I ask, suddenly worried something awful happened between them.

Thankfully, Harlow nods and offers me a soft smile. It's real and sincere and takes some of the toughness out of her features, replacing it with a sweetness I've yet to see her show. "Thank you, Zoe. Really. Things between Connor and me are crazy complicated. I don't even see him that often; just when Eli travels to Chicago and brings me along or when Connor comes out to L.A. Over the past year, that's been even less frequent. But, there's something about him…" She trails off, her eyes taking on a faraway shimmer.

I blow out a breath and commiserate with her. "It's the fighting. And the broodiness." I've seen it happen to more women than I can count, especially training up-and-coming MMA fighters working toward a title shot.

Harlow giggles, the sound unexpected coming from her. I realize that although we sort of clicked from the start, I really don't know her at all, but as our flight begins its descent, I'm glad our paths have crossed.

"I'm really happy you're here, Zoe," Harlow admits, as if reading my mind. "I don't have a lot of girlfriends. To be honest, you're like the first girl on Eli's team, besides me, that seems to dislike drama."

I wrinkle my nose. "No tolerance for that noise."

"Cheers to that." Harlow taps her champagne flute against mine and takes a sip.

Then we look at each other and laugh, our acquaintance blossoming into friendship by the time the plane's wheels touch down.

6

ELI

"Action!"

Immediately, I turn off any lingering thoughts as Eli Holt and embrace Dr. Henry Shorn, my character who becomes stranded on a remote island after living through a plane crash. He's the only survivor, heartbroken over the death of his fiancée and drowning in guilt over not being able to save her.

After rescuing one of the sons of an indigenous group from an explosion of the plane's wreckage, he becomes partially blind. As a result of his heroism, he's welcomed into the tribe's fold and ends up practicing medicine on a series of adventurous escapades with the natives until he falls in love with a woman from a rival group. In a few short months, Dr. Henry finds himself in a completely different reality from his swanky practice and quiet home life in Northern California.

"Are you okay?" I bend down, gently touching the ankle of a child. His character is the son of a local tribal leader.

He gestures with his hands, his eyes wide. Fearful.

"You're okay. I'm not going to hurt you. What's your name?" I gentle my tone, concern flooding my facial expression. "That's a nasty sprain." I attempt to doctor his ankle with what I have on hand – strips of my torn shirt and a handful of twigs.

"Ow!" he wails, his face contorting in pain. The strands of colorful beads around his neck shake as he hides his face behind his hands.

I scoop him up and hold him against my chest. "We've got to clean out those cuts."

"Wait!" he cries, lodging a hand against my chest.

"You speak English?"

He nods, lifting his hand and spreading his thumb and forefinger an inch apart. "Little bit. Who are you? Why you come here?"

"My name is Henry. I came here by accident. From the plane crash."

"We shouldn't be in the jungle."

I nod.

"We didn't find survivors."

Pain blazes across my face, my eyes filling with moisture. "I think I'm the only one."

"My name Siale. You take me home." He points in the direction of his home, but all I see is thick, green vegetation followed by white sand, and endless, endless sea.

"Tell me where to go."

"That way." He points again, and I start off toward the beach.

"Cut!" Preston's voice rings out.

Placing Josh onto his feet, he grins up at me.

I tousle his hair. "Nice job, buddy."

He grips my forearm with both of his, the beads adorning his wrists clacking against each other. "Thanks, Holt."

"Hungry?"

He nods. "I'm going to get a bagel."

"Me too." I follow him off set to the table prepared with an elaborate spread.

"Here." Harlow thrusts a hot cup of coffee in my hand, her eyes trained on Preston and his art director, Brian, as they re-watch some footage and discuss in hushed tones. "How far behind are you guys?"

"Few days."

"Damn."

"Yeah." I sip the coffee slowly, knowing Harlow has no concept of temperature since she drinks everything iced. Even wine. "How was your flight?"

"Fine."

My nostrils flare despite my best efforts to keep my mounting frustration at bay. Where the fuck is she? I want to ask, but I don't. I shouldn't care where Zoe is. She's just an employee, a member of my team.

But hell if I can't stop thinking about her. For the past four years, the one-night stands and casual hook-ups have worked really well for me. In fact, they're exactly what I wanted. Now, after just one night of exchanging barbs and jokes with a bartender from my hometown, I feel off-balance, yearning to know more about Zoe while fighting my ridiculous attraction to her.

Harlow chews the corner of her mouth, patiently waiting. She's going to make me say it.

Jesus. I have the best inner circle: tight, loyal, and honest. But damn if they don't test my patience.

"Zoe?" I clear my throat.

"Settled into room 322. Garden view. Exploring the hotel, particularly the gym, and the equipment, before meeting me for dinner." Harlow keeps her eyes trained on Preston. To give her a sliver of credit, she doesn't shoot me a smartass smirk or gloat while answering.

I glare at her, unsure if I feel relieved that she's already befriended Zoe or annoyed that she has more access to my new trainer than I do.

"What time?" I ask, irritated at the uptick of Harlow's lips. She's enjoying this. Watching me suffer. Watching me care about some random girl's plans.

"8PM."

"Where?"

"The Thai restaurant at the hotel."

"Add another one to the reservation." I gulp back more coffee, nodding as Preston turns, looking around for me.

"*Eli.*"

"What? She's a new member to my team. Shouldn't I at least welcome her?" I raise my eyebrows at Harlow.

"You didn't take me to dinner when I joined your team," she shoots back, but I can tell she's trying not to laugh.

"I barely had two pennies to rub together back then; I was the team. And if memory serves, I got you Taco Bell, so stop bitching."

Harlow snorts, her demeanor calmer than it usually is during the first few days of filming. "I'll add you to the reservation."

Pressing my coffee cup into her hands, I stride back to set, forcing the thoughts about Zoe's perfect ass and raven hair to fade from my mind.

I don't have time for distractions.

And she's proving to be the biggest one of all.

HARLOW: *Hey, sorry. I can't make dinner. Something came up. Be nice to Zoe.*

Shit. I wince as I re-read the message. I'd bet my life that

Harlow's cancellation has something to do with bullshit her mom's flinging at her. It's hard to believe someone as good as Low could be ripped from a womb so fucking rotten.

Pocketing my cell phone, I press the button for the elevator. As soon as I enter the restaurant, I spot Zoe. She's already seated at the table, her hair twisted up in a bun, wispy tendrils escaping. Her shoulders are bare, the slope of her neck graceful. Funky earrings hang from her earlobes, grazing her collarbone.

She's mesmerizing.

"I hear the mahi poke bowl is the thing to order here." I slide into one of the chairs at the four-person table in the center of Achara. Tapping a forefinger on the table, I roll a glance over Zoe's surprised face. "Harlow didn't tell you I was crashing?"

Zoe recovers. "She mentioned it, but I didn't think she was serious."

"She was. She also had to cancel."

"Is everything okay?"

"Yeah, I think it's something family-related." I pick up my linen napkin and drape it across my lap.

"Oh. Well, thank you." Zoe gestures toward the empty table. "But if you have other commitments, don't feel obligated to dine with me."

"I don't." I flag down a server. "Wine?"

"Um, sure."

"Red or white?"

"Red."

I rattle off the name of a bottle I like as Zoe looks on, bewildered.

She picks at the tablecloth nervously, her eyes darting around to the nearby tables, avoiding my gaze.

"No need to be nervous. Consider this a working dinner. A chance to welcome you to my team."

"Thanks." She picks up her water glass. "That's nice of you."

I reach out, placing a hand over hers until she looks up, her gaze finally meeting mine. "You want the truth? I was jealous that you and Harlow planned girl time without me. I'm really here for the apple martinis and advice on cuticle care. But then Harlow bailed so…"

"So you want me to fill you in on this season's hottest shade of blue?" She fills in the blank, her eyes shining.

"Exactly." I ease back in my chair, pulling my hand away from hers. "You settle in okay?"

"Yeah. Everything is really amazing. I've never been to a place like this."

"I know what you mean. I remember my first time on location. I had no idea what to expect and everything seemed so over-the-top, I was overwhelmed. It will take a few days to adjust to your new norm."

"Yeah. I can't believe we're here for four months."

"It goes by fast." I hold Zoe's wine glass out for the server to pour a taste test into. "What do you think?" I pass her the glass.

"Oh." She stiffens, surprise rippling over her face. She takes a small sip and literally groans as the wine hits her tongue, embarrassment flooding her features in the next moment. "It's really good."

"Glad you like it." I say as the server fills our glasses. "To your new adventure." I raise my glass in her direction.

"To your new film." She replies, clinking her glass against mine.

I take a long drink, while Zoe daintily takes a sip, her

eyes closing in pleasure, her skin flushed. I feel my dick twitch and my throat dry.

If I'm expected to sit across from her and stare at her soft skin and big eyes and be on my best behavior, I'll be drinking more than just wine. When it's time to order, I ask for the poke bowl while she opts for the pad woon sen.

Once the server disappears, Zoe's presence seems to expand, drawing all my attention to her. The back of my neck tingles and I crack it, not used to feeling this off-center in the presence of a woman. Any woman.

"Tell me about That Fit Bitch Life. How'd you get started?" I swirl my wine and lean back in my chair.

"It was a labor of love. For real." She admits, her face brightening. "I've always been into health and fitness. Well, since I was about eleven or twelve. My mom became very conscious of preparing healthy meals and I used to help her cook. We would explore different recipes, try new things to make the plate pop with color, or see how various spices blended together. Jumping into the fitness aspect was a natural progression. But my love for boxing and MMA came when I was about fifteen. My dad took me to one of the MMA gyms in Chicago and I just became enamored with the sport. The discipline, the dedication, the attention to every single detail in a bout. I jumped right in."

"Seriously? You used to do MMA?"

"Yeah." She smiles. "Boxing too."

"Tough girl."

Zoe flexes playfully. "Come on Holt, I'm super badass."

"Maybe until you preceded it with the word super."

She laughs, the sound musical and carefree. A woman at the table next to us glances over but Zoe doesn't even notice. I'm drawn to her and how uninhibited and natural she is. It's a refreshing change from the L.A. scene where women are constantly aware of everyone around them and how they fit into some social media moment.

"What about you?" She reaches into the breadbasket and swipes a roll. "Did you always want to be an actor?"

"Hell no." I take a drink of my wine. "I just wanted to get the hell out of my neighborhood."

Zoe flinches and for a moment I feel bad, remembering it's the same neighborhood she grew up in. "I hear that." She says softly, her expression turning thoughtful. "How'd you settle on L.A? Why not New York?"

"I wanted sunshine after a Chicago winter."

"Oh, that I definitely believe." She sips her wine, her shoulders relaxing. "Then what?"

"You know my story is public right? There's no secret about how I got my start."

Zoe wrinkles her nose. "I don't really read those magazines."

"No?"

"Nope." She pops the letter p. "I'm more of a Steinbeck girl."

Tossing my head back, I laugh. I mean, I really laugh and immediately she joins in. I like that about her, how easily she laughs, how naturally she blends in with whatever social setting surrounds her. Most girls would feel out of place trading their bartending shifts at a neighborhood pub with dining at a five-star restaurant overnight. But not Zoe. She could dazzle a gardener just as easily as an heiress. Something about her, her essence, is too bright to overlook.

In fact, as I listen to her share a funny anecdote about her boxing days, her face bright, her hands animated, I hate how unsure of myself I feel.

I hate how captivated I am by her, unable to look away.

On any other girl, her purple-infused hair would irk me as

a sign of rebellion or a cry for attention. On her, though, it intrigues me. Why does it have to look so natural? Like an extension of her personality? I can imagine that hair, silky and dark, spread across my pillow. Or better yet, fisted in my hand as those pouty lips take me down her throat.

Jesus Christ.

I shift in my chair to distract myself from my wayward, inappropriate, and completely honest thoughts. Zoe's gaze sharpens on mine, that ribbon of disguised interest I'm coming to count on in my interactions with her present in the butterscotch of her eyes.

In my next blink, the air between us shifts. The space intensifies, simultaneously constricting and expanding. My throat dries and my hands curl into fists.

Zoe's eyes darken and her tongue darts out to wet the center of her bottom lip.

I nearly groan, unable to tear my eyes away.

Her breathing ticks up the slightest bit, her perky tits straining against her white halter top. I can make out the faintest outline of her nipples and my dick twitches again.

"Zoe." I reach over the table, knowing it's the last thing I should do. The second my fingers touch the softness of her skin, I want more. My body craves hers, my fingers tingle to explore every inch of her curves. "I —"

"Your entrées." The server announces, breaking the spell between us.

I snap my hand back as he presents us with our meals.

Once he leaves, we're quiet, the sound of our breaths filling my ears. My eardrums ring with my pulse as I try and get a grip on the situation. In order to keep my relationship with Zoe somewhat professional, I'm going to have to keep her at arm's length. The best way to do that is to control the conversation. "Carb loading?" I clear my throat, teasing her as I nod toward her plate of noodles. But my tone lands like a jab instead of a joke, my body still reeling from several moments earlier when I was tempted, so goddamn tempted, to cross every single line in our professional relationship.

She flashes a smile, the corners of her mouth pinched. "Don't worry about me, Holt. I've got a rigorous training set up for you starting tomorrow." She says the words friendly enough, but the way she drops my last name, the same way everyone does, with a mixture of casual and condescending, ticks me off. I don't like it from her lips. Not when she could call me Eli.

Hell, even Hollywood.

"Don't give yourself too much credit, babe. It's early in the game." I slip back into default mode, arrogant jokester, saying anything to keep her where I want her, where I can get a read on her. I rub a hand over my chest, the material of my T-shirt rippling.

Her breath hitches in her throat as she follows my movement, her cheeks coloring. "What game is that?"

"The long game, baby girl. You just stepped into the majors. Sure you're ready for this?" I pester her, dropping my voice, dipping my head toward hers.

Her eyes widen before narrowing, accepting my challenge. She inches closer to me, slow and stealthy, like a damn cheetah. "More than ready, Hollywood. It's you who've taken on more than you can handle."

Snorting, amusement fills my tone. I like how brazen she is, how she never backs down. It keeps me in my place and throws me off-balance at the same time. "Is that right? I think I can handle you just fine, baby. All night long, 'til you're begging for more."

Aaaand there goes my professionalism. Again.

She gasps, her face turning the most brilliant shade of red. I wait for her to issue a witty retort, to call me on my shit.

Come on, Zoe. I need you to put me in my place.

"Hate to disappoint, Holt," she recovers, and relief flickers through me. "But a man like you could never handle a woman like me."

"Ouch," my grin widens as I drop a hand over my wounded heart. Ego. Same thing. "A man like me? What kind of a man do you take me for?"

Zoe giggles, her fingers pinching the stem of her wine glass as she takes another sip. "You missed the point, Hollywood. It really has nothing to do with what kind of a man you are. It's more about what kind of a woman I am. Most guys, yourself included, are always too focused on yourselves to see that it's not all about you." She winks, taking the sting out of her truth.

It's no secret that I'm arrogant, used to getting my way, and almost always the person in control. Especially in an exchange like this.

I never have to try this hard with a woman. To win her over or keep her at a distance.

Zoe's eyes glitter with satisfaction over the rim of her wine glass. She knows she's winning the banter game. She just flipped my entire argument on its head.

I finish my wine and Zoe's laughter, melodious, rings out.

"Don't take it so personal, Holt. I told you from day one, you would have crashed and burned. Besides, we're here to work." She reaches into the breadbasket for another roll. "Tomorrow, we're diving right in. I spoke with your trainer in L.A." She waggles her fingers at me like a little kid, and even that seems cute and not annoying. "I know all your weaknesses, and I'm going to make you sweat."

I breathe in a shaky breath, my grin tight. Why is this girl, my trainer, already under my skin? Already making me like her when the most important thing I need to do right now is keep my distance?

She's on your team.

She's on location.

She's off-limits.

As her chatter fills the air and her easygoing smile and friendly eyes scan the restaurant, I find myself unable to look away. Her energy, her glow, her mixture of sweetness and strength, thaws parts of me that I prefer to keep frozen.

"There he is." Preston drops a heavy hand on my shoulder as he walks past our table. "Hi." He smiles at Zoe, taking a step toward her and extending his hand. "I'm Gray Preston."

Zoe's smile is blinding, as radiant as the goddamn sun. I hate the way her face lights up as her gaze latches onto Gray's. "It's nice to meet you. I'm Zoe Clark, Eli's new trainer."

"Ah, yes. I heard you would be joining us." He dips his head toward me. "Do you have a moment when you guys are finished? I want to run something by you."

Before I can respond, Zoe answers. "We're nearly done."

"Excellent." Preston practically beams at her, his eyes wandering over her face for a beat longer than necessary.

My blood simmers through my veins. Is he into her? Did he really come over to speak with me or because he wanted to meet Zoe? Jesus, man, get a grip.

When I realize both Zoe and Gray are staring at me, I clear my throat, "Sorry?"

"Pop by my table when you're all done?" Gray asks, his brow furrowing.

"Of course. Give me fifteen."

"No rush." He turns toward Zoe again. "It was lovely to meet you Ms. Clark."

"Oh, call me Zoe."

"Only if you'll call me Gray."

Her smile widens and I swallow back bitterness. "It was great to meet you too, Gray."

Preston finally leaves and I indicate toward the server that I'll take the check.

"Wow." Zoe breathes out across from me and I feel my frustration heighten. "I can't believe that's Gray Preston."

"The one and only." I mutter, signing for our meal.

"Oh." Zoe reaches out a hand, her other fiddling with her purse. "You don't have to —"

"Get out of here, Violet." I dismiss her attempt to pay for her meal. Standing from the table, I glance at Preston, not sure if I'm relieved or irritated to be leaving Zoe to speak with him.

Zoe turns toward me as she stands, her lips curled upwards like she knows a secret I don't. Damn this woman. Why can't I get a pulse on her?

"See you tomorrow, Violet." I tug on the end of one of her purple streaks.

"Thank you for dinner, Holt. 6:45AM. Meet me on the beach."

I smirk in surprise. "The beach? Baby doll, I thought we were here to —"

"The beach, Holt. Don't be late. And don't forget your sunscreen. I hear you burn easily." She throws the last bit out like the ribbing it is, but as I stare at her, untouchable and unflappable, and my gaze catches on Preston, authoritative and dynamic, I feel like I'm floundering. Suddenly, her words ring like an insult in my ears. I shift my weight, a flicker of unease traveling through me.

I'm in over my head.

With this film.

With my career.

With my goddamn trainer.

"Bring your best, baby," I deflect, trying to find my footing.

"You're not ready for my best, Hollywood. But you will be."

7

ZOE

He rattles me. He knows it.

And he likes that he does it, making the nerves worse, the doubts larger, the stakes greater.

I've never backed down from a challenge before, and Eli Holt thrusts me into my next great upset like the cocky bastard he is.

The breeze coming off the water is still cool at this time in the morning. The morning glories of birds mix with the fading cheeps of nighttime critters. Wrapping my long-sleeve Lululemon sweater tighter around my waist, I scan the assortment of weights, ropes, and sliders I'm going to use for this morning's workout.

"You look beautiful." His voice runs over my skin like a caress, alerting me to his presence and sending my poor, unsuspecting body into a tailspin. Goosebumps skate over my skin, my stomach flip-flops, and my chest constricts.

Feigning casual, I snort and glance at him over my shoulder. "That work on all the girls?"

"Every last one." He's clad in black basketball shorts, a

teal workout tank that brightens the color of his eyes, and trainers.

"Not this one," I retort, nodding toward the weights. "We're going to circuit train today. I've got several stations set up. I'll run you through the exercise for each and the amount of reps you're required to do. I'll be timing you. The goal for each subsequent round is to beat your time. We're focusing on endurance and stamina."

"Got plenty of that, baby," he croons, a cocky expression on his perfectly sculpted face.

The breath from his words ripples across my body, more intense than the ocean breeze. I feel his words in every cell of my being, his gentle "baby" buzzing in their damn mitochondria. Deep down I know it's a lie; a cheap, generic quip to prove how much like all the other girls I really am to him.

Even though his words and the intent behind them makes certain parts of me burn up like winter leaves, I point to the first station. "Let's get started, Hollywood. We're on a schedule."

Once I launch into the exercises, he quits his fooling around and pays attention. I'm grateful for his focus because it makes it easier for me to draw a line in the sand.

The one that divides the professional and the personal.

The one that establishes the trainer-client relationship.

The one that reminds me that I can admire his rugged good looks and sculpted body all day long, but underneath those corded muscles is a cavalier man used to getting everything he wants, women included.

Gripping my stopwatch, I call out, "Start."

Eli begins the first set of side-to-side kettlebell swings before dropping the weight and sprinting to the second station. After his first round, I nod, impressed with his times.

"You did good, Holt. Really great times on stations two and three."

"Is this your best, Violet?" he taunts.

"Not even close. You need to run it three more times. Here." I chuck a bottle of water at his head.

He catches it easily, smirking as he downs half its contents.

"Get ready to go again."

Eli runs through the circuit three more times. By the final round, his numbers have dipped, as expected. Sweat pours down his back, drips from his eyebrows, trails down his neck. His shirt has darkened, clinging to his chest and abdomen like a second skin.

Rugged, disheveled, and sexy as hell, Eli Holt looks like every woman's fantasy. Strong, resilient, and determined. The blaze of his eyes, brimming with a fortitude that fills up so many of the searching places inside me, centers me. He possesses the overwhelming commitment to do whatever is expected of him, and then do it better. He's focused, centered, in complete control of himself and everything surrounding him. His drive mirrors my own, and I recognize it instantly, drawn to his ambition.

He's a trainer's dream client. A woman's fantasy. And the greatest downfall to a girl with nothing to lose.

All wrapped in one, like a present. I want to pick at the paper, unwrapping him slowly, one strand at a time. Savoring each inch of the experience. Building up the hype. Because the opening of this gift almost, *almost*, promises to be better than the present itself.

"You can take a picture, Violet," he says, mopping his face with a towel.

"Nah, photos don't do your type of discipline justice."

He jerks at the genuine compliment, stepping toward me and dropping the towel. Rivulets of sweat and salt and every pheromone in the universe cling to his skin as he studies me. His eyes are thoughtful, momentarily devoid of their constant assuredness, and he looks more beautiful than I've ever seen him.

"I didn't hate today," he finally says.

"I'll see what I can do so you don't shit on tomorrow."

The right side of his mouth lifts, an almost-smile. Even in the short amount of time I've spent in his presence, I recognize this as the truest of his smiles. When he grins, it's patronizing. When he chuckles, an insult is coming.

But when he offers the briefest, smallest, facial flicker, it's sincere. Kind of like him. Flashy, forward, easily affable on the outside, but deep down, closed off, cautious, and incredibly fickle.

"Tomorrow then?" he grunts, picking up a bottle of water and uncapping it.

"See you then, Hollywood."

Eli nods once before walking down the beach, back toward the hotel.

As much as I hate to admit it, I watch his every step with a strange sense of longing. Like I'm missing something I never had to begin with.

"How'd this morning go?" Harlow asks when I enter the lobby of the hotel.

"Not bad. Eli showed up to work. All okay with you?" I take the seat beside her.

She sighs. "Yeah. Sorry about skipping dinner last night.

Something came up with my mom." She shifts her weight in her chair, her grip on her book tightening.

"No worries. As long as you're good." I nod toward her book. "What're you reading?"

She sighs, a sheepish expression crossing her face and flashes me the title.

Reclaiming Brave.

"Romance?" I guess, checking out the couple on the cover.

"This," she shakes the paperback, "is the only action I'm getting. I blame Connor."

"Wait… you're that hung up on him?" Surprise rolls through me as I realize just how much my new friend likes Connor Scott. And, from what I do know about him, he probably has no clue.

"I know. It's pathetic."

"It's not. It's just," I blow out an exhale, trying to find the right words, "relationships are hard."

Harlow cracks a smile. "Have you had many?"

"Relationships? No."

"Why not?"

"Too damn hard." I decide to keep the real reason, the one buried so deep in my soul it's sometimes a secret even to myself, hidden. I tap the cover of her book, "Sometimes I think we're better off with these. A guaranteed happily-ever-after."

Harlow laughs, but the shadow that appeared in her eyes at the mention of Connor lingers.

"Come on." I stand, pulling her up beside me. "Let's grab a coffee. Next week we should head into town, find a local spot, and do a real girls' night with colorful cocktails and dancing."

"That sounds perfect," Harlow agrees, and I can tell she means it. "Café's this way."

At ease and grateful to have made a friend in this new, strangely convoluted world, I follow her toward the caffeine.

8

ELI

"Good morning, Hollywood." Her voice is straight whiskey, husky and smoky and smooth.

"How's it going, Violet?" I stride onto the beach, scanning the various workout equipment Zoe has set up. My chest swells with the challenge I foresee; today's workout is going to kick my ass.

I don't know if this girl is trying to prove something to me or herself with these insane circuits, but no way in hell am I backing down. On a personal level, I'll disappoint her seven ways to Sunday, but I won't compromise the integrity of my character or my commitment to this film.

"Oh you know, just enjoying how the other half live." She gestures to the calm sea lapping against the shoreline, all blue-green water and sunlight.

"More like one-percent." I dip down to tie my laces.

"It's pretty incredible." Her voice is wistful. When I stand, she's staring at the horizon, her thoughts taking her far away from the moment. Longing shadows her face, her mouth twisting.

Frowning, I step forward, my eyes drinking in her expression like a desert wanderer, desperate to understand it before she blinks and hides behind the cheery facade she's got going on. At my movement, she turns, her expression turning sheepish.

"Penny for your thoughts," I press my luck.

She smiles, soft and sweet, the corners of her mouth turning up the tiniest bit. "You're doing an incredible job on this film."

My nostrils flare at the lie that easily slips through her lips. She doesn't want to be honest with me. I get it, I'm rarely honest with anyone. Still, her haunting expression, and her unwillingness to talk about it, spikes my curiosity.

I'm nothing if not a pain in the ass.

"How do you know that?" I ask instead, turning away to stretch.

"I came to set yesterday."

That gets my attention. Spinning around, I glare at her. "Why?"

"Why?"

"Yeah. Why were you on set?"

"Oh, I brought Harlow a smoothie." She shrugs, her face contorted in confusion.

"Whatever," I grumble, shaking my head.

I don't know why the thought of her on set unnerves me. Dozens of people are swarming around, watching, not watching, preparing, all of it. But the thought of Zoe seeing me as Henry Shorn agitates me. I haven't perfected him yet, and I'm not a hundred percent sure of the way I'm playing him. I don't want her assessing eyes, which seem to see more than I want her to, to witness me in a moment of weakness while I'm trying to vault my most challenging professional hurdle to date.

"Okay." She claps her hands, ending the awkwardness.

"Let me run you through today." She explains the different stations she set up and I nod, understanding all the exercises.

I run her circuit three times, the exercises challenging as hell but successful in distracting me from my thoughts. My mind goes blissfully blank, my body taking over as I perform each exercise, commit to each set, dig into each repetition with all my mental focus on the task at hand. When I'm done, sweat dripping off of me in waves, hunched forward, my hands braced on my knees, trying to catch my breath, Zoe's shoes appear in my line of vision.

I straighten and she passes me a bottle of water, the cap screwed off.

"Thanks." I murmur, guzzling the water as my heart rate slowly returns to normal.

"You killed that." Her voice is soft, a thread of admiration in her tone.

Nodding off the compliment, I take a few steps away, trying to burn off the energy that spikes inside me from her presence.

"I'm serious. I've trained a lot of guys, mostly in the MMA circuit. They're brutal, absolute beasts at hitting the weights and the bags. But your body is lean and agile, quick and smooth. Nice work, Hollywood."

Peering at her from the corner of my eye, I sense her honesty. A part of me wonders about the other guys she trains, the brutal beasts. Do they hit on her? Does she date them? Does she even have a boyfriend?

"You single, Violet?"

She glances at me. "What?"

"Do you have a boyfriend?" I don't even care what she thinks at this point, I just need to know that the answer is no.

She shakes her head, that twisted yearning, laced with anguish, washing over her face again. "No."

Her answer should be a relief but it's not because her expression when she says no bothers me.

Bad breakup?

Pining for some asshole juiced up on steroids?

Her posture, defeated shoulders curling in on herself, is a far cry from her usual assuredness. Whoever the asshole is for hurting her, I hate him.

First for putting her through whatever hell she's in.

And second, for having her at all to break her like this.

Dr. Henry Shorn is the most complicated character I've ever played.

That's not really saying much, as my other characters were glorified man candy.

Sure, I had lines. I just don't know if anyone listened to them once my shirt came off.

But Henry Shorn, jack of all trades, successful physician, fiancé to Sara, lover of anthropology and reader of newspapers, has layers. The kind that require constant attention to detail and daily practice.

Running lines alone is sometimes better than practicing with someone because it allows me the time to brainstorm different facial expressions, tone inflections, and appearances.

Sitting on a chair in a tiny enclave by the beach, the scent of Zoe's perfume assaults my nose. It's not sweet and fruity, or musky and earthy, but something in between. Something uniquely her. A mixture of sweet and spice and sass.

Jesus Christ. This girl is invading my senses now.

When I catch a glimpse of her dark hair and hear the rustle of her dress, I clear my throat.

She spins around, a smile touching her lips when she sees

me. "Hey," she calls, walking around the greenery and flowers, grinning like we're old friends. Like she's happy to see me. Is she? "What're you doing out here?"

"Running lines. Been practicing facial expressions." I pluck at the skin next to my eyebrow. I'm not making much progress, but no way am I admitting that to her.

"Having a hard time remembering how to take off your shirt?" The question is innocent, but her eyes burn with mischief.

"You suck, Violet." I toss the script down on the cafe table and lean back in my chair.

"Wouldn't you like to know how hard, Hollywood?" she asks coyly, tilting her head.

I sputter. Literally choke on my own spit. "What the fuck?"

She grins cheekily. "Just giving it as good as you, sweetheart," she murmurs, her voice deep and husky, scrubbing a hand over the lower portion of her face.

I point at her. "Is that supposed to be me?"

She collapses, uninvited, into the chair on the other side of the table, one armrest against her back, her knees hooked over the other armrest. "Think I nailed ya, Hollywood."

I laugh. A genuine laugh. Shaking my head, I flip her the middle finger.

"Wow. A real laugh." She bats her eyelashes, ignoring my middle finger by subtly scratching her nose with hers. "Something to write home about."

"What? You mean the five-star hotel, Michelin chef meals, and freaking perfumed hibiscus flowers aren't enough?"

"You know," she gestures to the beach surrounding us, "I never thought this would be my life."

"Yeah, well, it's not always as magical as it seems."

"Nothing ever is."

"The perception is always different than the reality." I cross my arms over my chest. "When I first moved from Chicago to L.A., I thought I had made it. Big houses, cars that actually started when you flipped the ignition, a fully stocked fridge, it seemed like a dream." I bite my tongue, not sure why I'm telling her this. It's not like my humble beginnings are a secret, it's just that I don't usually talk about them. At least not with anyone outside my inner circle: Evan, Connor, and Harlow. And rarely Harlow. She just learned by being a bystander in all my major life interactions for the past four years.

"But sometimes you miss the simplicity of not having it all," Zoe states quietly, not a question at all.

"Yeah."

"What's the deal with your character?" She flips her chin at the rolled script in between us.

"He goes partially blind after saving one of the local kids from playing in the abandoned plane. A bunch of the kids are playing in the wreckage and an explosion occurs and he saves one of the kids, Siale. It's how he gains the trust of the local community, but it costs him his vision. Not all of it, but enough to change the way he interacts with people, his understanding of depth, his outlook."

"You need to nail the subtleties."

"What?"

"The little things. That's what you should focus on. That's what will make a difference to how he appears on screen. How did this alluring, engaging, Renaissance man who survived a plane crash and walked off with a few scratches become a man petrified to leave the side of a stranger to pee? He was once admired for his looks, but now he can't see himself in a mirror, or the reflection of water.

The sound of the crashing waves is too loud for him, the dips in the sand aren't uneven but pits of quicksand. What does he do when he reaches the ocean? Does he go in or freeze? How does he shave in the morning? How do sounds affect his new reality?" She taps the top page of the script. "You need to nail the subtleties. That's what will define this role for you. Not the actions, but the emotions behind them. You need to project the fear, the isolation, the questioning of all the unimportant details that now rule your character's mind."

I hunch forward in my chair, intrigued and curious and a thousand more things I don't want to be. "How do you know this?"

Zoe sighs, glancing out toward the beach. "My dad. He lost some of his vision, about forty percent, thirteen years ago. Since then, it's been steadily getting worse. Now, he only has about twenty percent left."

My stomach twists as I take in Zoe's heartbroken expression, hear the break in her voice when she mentions her dad. I feel my throat thicken, and the desire to reach out and touch her hand overwhelms me, but I hold back.

"How?"

"A chemical accident. He worked at the chemical plant outside the city."

"Damn. That blows, Zoe."

"No one knows how hard it's been for him. How big the fear is and how crippling the isolation can be. He's... my dad's the bravest guy I know. He never backs down from anything. Instead of wallowing in pity, he lifts everyone around him up. That's why he bought Shooters and took it over."

"Wait." I hold up a hand. "Your dad owns Shooters? Your dad's Joe Clark?"

Zoe nods, biting the corner of her mouth. "You know him?"

"Hell yeah, I know him. I mean, I don't know him, know him, but I've met him a time or two. I've been coming to Shooters a long time. I usually see him when I pop in for a beer whenever I'm in town. I knew he had a daughter, but —" I shake my head, my eyes scanning Zoe, "well, I had no clue it was you. I guess I should have put two and two together, your last name also being Clark. How's he doing?"

Zoe sighs, "Shooters is his baby now. He pours all his energy into that bar. He's there every day, gossiping with regulars about his aches and pains and talking football stats with anyone who will listen. That's what he did with the bit of insurance money he fought two years for." She rolls her eyes. "In the beginning, it was obviously devastating. My mom went with him to all of his therapy sessions and doctor's appointments. They even looked into clinical trials at Massachusetts General. When she couldn't anymore, I started filling out his paperwork, reading his exercise list to him. Watching him stumble, cheering on his triumphs. I know how he cocks his head when he's trying to gauge how close a sound is. I know not to move furniture, even the slightest bit, when I'm cleaning his house because it could result in a fall. I know he now feels safer out at night than during the day, which makes no sense but still rings true because it's quieter. More peaceful. Those are the subtleties you need to perfect."

"Why can't your mom help out and drive your dad anymore?" I question, picking up on the only part of her story that doesn't pertain to me. Instead of letting it go like I would with anyone else, I demand more information.

Zoe averts her gaze to pick at a cuticle. "She passed when I was thirteen. Breast cancer."

Closing my eyes, I blow out a deep breath.

Fuck.

This girl, this beautiful, optimistic girl who breathes sunshine and rainbows and hustles like there isn't going to be a tomorrow, knows the fragility of life. And owns it like the purple streaks woven through her hair.

"Don't feel bad for me, Hollywood." My nickname on her lips sounds more personal, intimate even, now that I know her backstory. "My family, we do okay for ourselves. We never had much, but the moments we did were filled with light and love. The type that fills up all your empty spaces and gives you something to hang onto when darkness comes. Don't pity me for a single second."

Opening my eyes, I swallow. "I'm not."

Zoe pauses, studying me intently for a long beat. "Do you trust me?"

9
ZOE

Eli's eyes are dark, like the sky right before a thunderstorm. Storm clouds pass over his irises, moving like shadows. The lines in his face harden, his mouth firm. "I could." The words drop from his lips like a confession, surprise sparking in his irises.

"You could," I repeat, rummaging into my bag to pull out the sleep mask I acquired from my only flight in business class.

Eli chuckles, the flash of vulnerability from a moment earlier buried deep once more. "Why didn't you tell me you wanted to play, babe?"

I roll my eyes and fling the sleep mask at him. "Who says I need you to play?"

He laughs, amusement stamping out the unease in his eyes. The corners of his mouth curl up the tiniest bit. I relish the fact that I can make him relax, let down his guard, and be present in the moment. It's no secret that this guy oozes confidence and sex appeal in spades.

He also armors himself in a shield of good time fun and

relies on digs or humor to keep everyone at arm's length from the real him.

The fact that little, quirky, nobody Zoe can make a man like Hollywood laugh bolsters my confidence. It rolls around the inside of my mouth like candy, dissipating before I can swallow, but hitting me like a high. "Cover your eyes."

"Why?" He grins wider, his eyes trained on mine.

"It's to help Dr. Henry Shorn. You need to learn how your other senses heighten when one is taken away. When you can't see, your sense of hearing, of smell, the importance of touch will all have a greater value to you."

"That makes sense." Eli agrees, his gaze dipping to my mouth and back up again. "You're not going to lead me to the ocean and push me in, right?"

Gah! *Is he actually flirting with me?* "Don't give me any ideas, Hollywood. Hey, shouldn't you have an acting coach or a professional to help you with this?" I stand from my chair, tipping my head toward the ocean.

Eli nods, grumbling under his breath as he stands next to me.

"What?" I press.

"Fired him."

"Already? And here I thought working with you was going to be a picnic."

"What happened to anything worth achieving not being that easy?" Eli asks, quirking an eyebrow.

I smile, glancing up at him to shoot off something casual and breezy but when I meet his gaze, something shifts between us. The playfulness from moments ago disappears, an intensity I'm unprepared to process taking its place.

His eyes blaze with something I can't decipher. The skin around his mouth tightens, a small muscle in his jaw ticks.

His expression, a mixture of fury and vulnerability, wars with itself.

His looks are lethal on a good day. In a moment like this, they're brutal.

I drown in his eyes, begging them with mine to let me in.

We're alike, Hollywood and me. We both yearn for something we can't have, and we both try to disguise our desires with laughter and humor, good times, and easy quips.

We don't trust easily and it doesn't matter, because we'll never admit that we want to.

The air around us crackles with a heat that threatens to burn us both if we step any closer. Ocean waves lap in the background, exotic birds chirp in harmony with the stridulation of a thousand crickets. My skin tingles and my body tightens with awareness.

The breeze whispering against my bare shoulders. The material of my dress suddenly restrictive, my breasts pressing against it. The need gathering low in my abdomen, seeping into my core.

Jeez Louise.

I want Eli Holt. Want him in ways I've never wanted a man.

I don't just want his body. I want his attention. I want his praise. I want all the cocky and conceited words that fall from his lips so I can spin them around in my own mind and read something deeper in the codes he spits.

His eyes flair, a wild concoction of desperation and defiance that begs me closer while warning me away. It's heady and dangerous.

His hands dart out, fastening around my hips as he pulls me closer, until I'm flush against him, our chests heaving in rhythm. His hands are splayed wide, his fingers nearly touching my spine as he squeezes. "Violet." His voice is a curse. "You're too damn shiny for my world." He says the words as if he knows my thoughts, as if he understands that moments ago, I lost all sense of reality.

My mouth dries, my hands tentatively reach up, fingertips dragging across his chest. "I thought your world was all sparkle and glamor."

The corner of his mouth twitches, his eyes so dark that his pupils bleed into his irises. Hypnotizing. "My world is cheap glitter, babe. But you're the brightest glow I've ever seen. I'll taint you, stamp out your bright with my dark, bend your straight, and tarnish your shiny. I can only dull a brightness like yours. Ask around. Look at the magazine covers. I never stick around."

Working a swallow, I try to settle the inferno in my bloodstream. His words don't stop my need. No, they intensify it. For what? So I can try to prove him wrong? "Who says I want someone to stick around?"

He jerks back an inch, the muscles under my fingertips tightening. "Eventually, someone always wants that." His voice is quiet, his breath, cool mint with a trace of whiskey washes over my face.

Shivers shimmy down my spine as goosebumps break out over my skin. Desperately needing space before I go and do the most reckless thing I can think of, before I give Eli the tiny inch that will undoubtedly result in the entire mile, I cling to my humor with both hands. "If I'm supposed to believe what the magazines print about you, do you want me to embrace the sex god stories too?"

The corner of his mouth lifts. Up, up, up, into a half smirk. "I like you Violet. More than I should. You always say the most unexpected things. As much as I mess with you, you captivate me. And for the record, the acting coach was a dick.

Grabbed Harlow's ass while she was buttering a bagel for Josh. Can't have that shit going on around here."

My heart stutters over his words, swelling until it nearly bursts.

I captivate him?

Who is Eli Holt? Sexy heartbreaker, broody actor, arrogant jokester, secret Good Samaritan?

Is it sad that I'm impressed by his response? That it's not just the obvious thing to do — fire the asshole for feeling up a woman?

But in this circle, even I know it's not. It makes my respect for the sex god increase a notch.

"Sounds like a dick."

"The smallest." Eli drops his hands from my waist. Immediately, I feel the loss of his heat and have to force myself not to lean into him. "Okay, we'll do this your way."

"You can remove the mask if you feel uncomfortable. Let's just take a walk on the beach."

His eyes cut to mine, his face softening with a trace of vulnerability even though his eyes heat with a hunger that yearns in its intensity.

Everything between us flickers to life. An energy that pulls me to Eli even though my common sense and his own words warn me away.

He slips the mask over his eyes, swiping his tongue across his bottom lip. I nearly groan at the visual. The one unfolding in my mind like a fantasy. Eli stripped naked in bed, me straddling him. He reaches up to —

Jeez Louise, girl. Get it together.

Stepping forward, I wave a hand in front of his face.

"What are you doing?" His voice is low.

"Making sure you can't see."

Eli chuckles, low and rumbly. It does things to my insides. "I feel the air moving from your hand."

"Good. Employ your other senses." I drop my hand, steel my shoulders, and take a deep breath.

Then, I reach out and lace my fingers with Eli's, pleased by the catch in his breath. "I'm going to lead you down to the beach. Anything you sense, feel, smell, whatever, just say it out loud. Okay?"

"Okay." He adjusts his grip on my hand, pressing our palms together.

I lead him through the garden, toward the water.

"The lapping of the waves," he breathes out. "The salt in the air. Music is playing far off, probably at the bar inside the hotel. I think it's going to rain."

"Why?"

"I can smell it in the air. It's too…heavy."

"Good. What else?"

"The air is cooler down here, closer to the water. The sand, it's like I can feel every grain against my feet."

We walk in silence as we approach the sea. I squeeze his hand once, then drop it. "Take a minute to walk on your own. Think about how you feel, how your surroundings are. I won't let you drown."

He offers me a quick smile. A moment later, his face turns serious, his stance alert. Sensing. Searching.

He's actually taking my lesson seriously, focusing on this moment. On his senses. The realization fills me with pleasure. It also offers me a rare opportunity to study him uninterrupted.

Looking at Eli in person is completely different from seeing his face on a magazine or his hot body in an Instagram post. There are nuances that the media doesn't capture.

Maybe it's because he's hiding pieces of himself. Or maybe because he really is that complex.

His jawline smooths out in the moonlight. His full mouth is straight with concentration but soft, losing the firmness of earlier. His arms drop an inch, relaxation rippling through his shoulder blades instead of the tension he usually holds there. His pace is languid, an appreciation in each step as he isn't hurrying through the tasks of his normal day.

The ocean moves closer, water rushing over his toes and he inhales, surprise twisting his mouth.

Suddenly, I wish I could see his eyes, read the emotions flitting between the shadows of his thoughts.

"You'll follow me, Violet?"

"Right behind you, Hollywood," I assure him, trailing him down the beach as he loses more and more of his concentration to this exercise.

Several paces from a jetty, he winces, his foot catching on a rock.

"We're nearing the jetty." I call out.

He nods, stopping in place. Reaching down, he grasps a handful of wet sand, rubbing it between his fingers, bringing it to his nose and inhaling deeply. His back stretches from the movement, the T-shirt hugging his muscles pulled taut.

God, he's tall. I could wear five-inch heels and just reach his chin. The thought causes shivers to shimmy down my arms.

I roll my eyes at myself.

Dropping the sand, Eli brushes his wet hands against his jeans and turns, pulling off the mask.

For a blink, I catch his unguarded expression, witness the surprise of what he's learned, the solemnity of what that means, and the gratitude for this new experience to shine between us in the glow of the moon.

10

ELI

Her expression is expectant.

Not with demands, or unfulfilled obligations, but to see if I learned from her exercise, to see if she helped me in some way.

Her face is open and candid and so damn vulnerable it pisses me off almost as much as I want to protect it. Protect her against all the bullshit that will erode at her trust.

Especially in my world.

"Did it help?" Her voice is small, a quiver in the dark night. But her presence looms in the center of the beach, lit up by moonlight, brightened by her simple but seductive white dress. She's playing with fire and has no idea the type of burn I'll leave.

"Yes," I admit, the word ripping from my throat against my wishes.

She smiles, her expression blossoming like a sunflower. Because I offered her a gleam of hope where none exists.

Not for me.

Not for us.

"Good. I'm glad." Her voice is huskier, slightly breathless.

Nodding, I step closer. The salt from the sea hangs heavy in the air around us. A shiver runs over Violet's skin. I bite my lip, wondering if it's from the breeze or my proximity.

Walk away, Holt. Let her go. Natalie already tarnished whatever good you had to give.

Don't get involved with another woman. They all look pretty and shiny. They all hide secrets and lies.

But when I look at Zoe, I don't see any of the malicious intents of Natalie Beck.

Then again, I never saw them with her either. Not until it was too late.

"I don't trust myself around you, Violet." I offer her the words, a pathetic attempt to explain the things I refuse to admit out loud.

"Why?" she whispers.

"Because I'll only end up letting you down."

"You don't know that."

"I do. I'll let you down because I'll never want more than the moment. Than the now. And eventually, you will."

"Did you think I was joking earlier? You're giving yourself a lot of credit here, Hollywood."

Smirking, my hands settle on her hips once more. My fingers rub the flimsy fabric of her dress, pulling it taut. I want to rip it from her body, lay her down on the white sand, and take everything she offers.

I won't take her slowly. And it sure as fuck won't be sweet.

I want to devour her in a carnal way that imprints on the backs of her eyelids, so every time she closes her eyes, each fucking blink, she sees me. I will ruin her for every man who comes afterwards. Consume her entirely until she combusts, the only proof of my pillage a goddamn sand angel, to be drowned in the sea before dawn.

"Then prove me wrong, Violet." It's the last out I give her, a small pause. A gasp drops from her lips. Her eyes shine, a glorious gold that will undoubtedly dim the longer she knows me.

It's subtle, the way her back arches. The flutter of her eyelashes, small half-moon shadows brushing against the delicate curve of her cheeks.

It's everything. It's the permission I need to drop my head and take. Drink the sweetness of her intentions. Steal the light that resides in her soul.

Corrupt her brightness and let it meld with all the dark that fills the cavity of my chest.

I fuse my mouth to her lips, run my hands up her back until my fingertips grip the strands of her hair, and swipe my tongue against the seam of her lips, demanding entry.

She sighs, her mouth opening, her chest pressing into my abdomen, her tight nipples rubbing against my T-shirt, creating a friction she loves because she moans.

And that's the tipping point.

My tongue clashes with hers, hot, heady, and so goddamn desperate. Our movements aren't fluid or natural. They're nearly disjointed with the need to suck every damn sensation from her, from this moment, from the now.

She grips my shoulders, moving her hands to the back of my neck. Her fingernails score my scalp and I grin, biting down on her tongue.

"Fuck." It falls from her mouth, surprising both of us.

In the next beat, I grip her ass with one hand, my other forearm bracing against her spine as I lift her into my arms. "Give me everything, Violet," I command, taunting her until she hooks her elbows over my shoulders and hoists herself up, taking charge.

Our kiss is a battle of wills. A duel between light and dark. A promise and a threat and the foreshadowing of disaster.

Right now, though, I let the sensations of her mouth, the boldness of her touch, block everything out.

Laying her on the white sand, I crawl up her body, raking her dress up until it's pushed over her breasts.

Fuck.

She's perfect. All creamy skin and delicious curves. Dragging my tongue up the center of her stomach, she arches off the sand. I don't waste any time pulling down the cup of her bra, and greedily fasten my mouth over her nipple, licking and sucking until she moans. Then I switch to her other breast. Beneath me, Zoe gasps, her legs winding around my back and hooking, heels digging into me.

"Oh God, Eli," she murmurs.

My name, dropping from her mouth, works through the fog in my head and douses me in a bucket of cold water.

Why the fuck did she have to go and do that? Say my name when all she's been doing is calling me Holt or Hollywood?

I could ruin her when she made me feel casual.

But not now. Not when she's already unknowingly messing with my head. Giving me more of herself than just the surface, confiding in me about her family, helping me with my lines. Violet's generosity is unexpected at face value, but even more so because I can't find the motive behind it. That makes her dangerous to a guy like me.

A man who once gave himself so whole-heartedly, with blind trust and desperate hopes, that the destruction from that failed relationship is irreparable. I'll never be whole again, and I'll never stop yearning for that wholeness.

Sliding off of her, I kneel, the damp sand pressing into my shins. She rises onto one elbow, looking at me with concern, not anger, in her eyes.

And that infuriates me. It makes the desire in my blood flare into anger. I want her to rake me over the coals for being a goddamn pussy and not drilling into her right here at the ocean's edge.

Instead, her honey eyes bleed with a tender compassion that rips through my chest, causing my breath to stutter.

"Get up." I stand, tearing my gaze from her perfect body.

She's standing next to me in an instant, her hair a wild mess, splotches of red coloring her face and neck from where my stubble rubbed against her. She looks worked the fuck over.

Like some arrogant dick had his way with her.

"What's wrong?" she asks, her breathing ragged. Her finger reaches out to touch mine and I jerk my hand away.

"This was a mistake. You work for me. Jesus." I dig the heels of my palms into my eyes and lie through my teeth. "I need to focus on this film. I can't fuck someone on my damn team. The last thing I need is a sexual harassment charge."

Her brows furrow. "What? I'd never — that was consensual," she says, a blush blazing over her cheeks. Averting her gaze, she shakes her head. "You know what, forget it. You're right. This was a mistake. I'm here to do a job, and I won't jeopardize my family trying to decipher your mixed messages. Good luck tomorrow, Holt."

I wince at the barrier she erected between us even though I caused it. Wanted it.

Watching her walk up the beach and back to the hotel, I swear under my breath.

My body protests her departure, my dick lashing out at me for being so fucking stupid.

My bright spot disappears. I'm left alone with my angry thoughts, my sinister intentions, and the peaceful sound of waves ringing in my ears.

AFTER EVERYTHING WITH ZOE, sleep doesn't find me. I'm almost grateful when Evan's FaceTime call comes at the ungodly hour of 3AM.

"Shit, man." He winces when he sees me. "Forgot about the time change."

"Can't sleep anyway," I admit, scraping a hand over my face. I pull myself from bed, tug on a pair of sweatpants, and relocate to the living room. "What's going on?"

"Not much. Ollie's soccer team won their game this week."

"Yeah? That's awesome. Did the little man score any goals?"

"Two."

I don't miss the pride in Evan's voice. A type of pride I'll never fully understand, an honor I'll never know.

"I guess things are popping off for you too, huh?" he adds. "Why didn't you tell me?"

"What are you talking about?" No way he already found out about my little beach escapade with Zoe. But damn, paparazzi are everywhere these days. It's called a teenage punk with an iPhone.

"About Brooke Silver. She's going to be staring opposite Dr. Henry Shorn in Gray Preston's new film, *Dangerous Devils*."

"Ah, yes, it wasn't confirmed until two days ago. Madeline was hoping she'd be able to film in time, but things went a little sideways with her pregnancy, so Gray and the casting director reached out to Brooke."

My brother shakes his head, shooting me a look. "That's not going to be awkward for you?"

"No." I slide my fingers through my hair. "Brooke and I barely dated. It was, what, three months? And we parted on good terms, knowing we weren't what the other was looking for. If anything, we've maintained a friendship. Working with her will probably be easier than working with Madeline since I know Brooke so well."

Evan laughs. "Your life is so weird sometimes."

It must seem that way to him and Connor. How I've dated women one week and worked with them the next. It's the norm in my industry, in my life, and it stopped being jarring years ago. Sometimes I wish for the simplicity of having a real partner, of knowing I can come home at the end of a long day to a woman who accepts me for me.

I've never had that, not even with Natalie. And now, I've come to terms with the fact that I never will.

"How are things going with Preston?"

"They're fine. Yeah, the film is coming along. Preston's been nothing but professional. Our working relationship seems solid. In fact, Natalie's name hasn't come up once."

"Good. And your character?"

"He's a bit more complicated," I admit, scrubbing a hand over my face. "But Zoe helped me out tonight with running lines."

"The bartender?"

"Yeah, she's Joe Clark's daughter."

"I know." Evan looks at me like I'm an idiot for not piecing that one together.

I shrug, "Well, my character deals with blindness so…"

"Ah, gotcha. Well, hey, that worked out even better than you anticipated, huh? Helping out someone local, her being a great trainer, and even helping you with your character."

"Yeah."

Evan's quiet as he studies me for a long moment, "Don't go starting anything with her, Eli."

"What? I'm not."

"Maybe not yet. But you're thinking about it."

I snort, shaking my head at my brother.

"I know you. And you like her. You've liked her from the moment you met her."

"She's different," I admit.

"She's also on your team, and you're filming the biggest movie of your career."

"Yeah." I nod. "Yeah, you're right."

"You've worked too long for this opportunity, Eli. Now's not the time to lose your head over a girl."

"I know; I'm not. It's just an attraction, that's all. Like if I could just get her out of my system, I'd be over it. But I can't even do that since she's my goddamn trainer."

"You want her because you can't have her."

"Exactly."

"Well, figure out another way to get over it. Run more."

I chuckle, shaking my head at my brother. "Yeah, I don't think that's going to work. But really, it's nothing. Tell me more about Ollie." I kick back, bending my arm beneath my head as Evan fills me in on the gossip circulating in Ollie's first-grade class.

We talk for another fifteen minutes before I disconnect the call and pull myself up from the couch. I stroll through my intricately decorated, plush suite that echoes with loneliness, throw myself back into my eight-thousand thread count Egyptian cotton sheets, and beg for sleep.

11

ZOE

"Brooke Silver is going to be here in two days. I know there's been a low profile with media coverage, but that's about to change."

My stomach sinks and sours. Brooke Silver. Supermodel. Actress. Eli Holt's ex-girlfriend. News broke yesterday that she was replacing Eli's original co-star and would arrive in the Seychelles this week.

The entire situation is a tough pill to swallow, especially when I can still feel the stubble of Eli's jawline pressing into my stomach. I can still breathe in the scent of his cologne mixed with ocean and wind and hold it in my lungs. I can still get completely and totally lost in his kiss, *the kiss*, that made me feel more in five seconds than I did in my entire five-month relationship with Chris Johnson.

Le sigh.

"Did you hear me?" Harlow bumps my shoulder with hers.

"Yeah. Brooke Silver."

"She's, like, on another level of famous. She's been in the industry since she was a kid. The paparazzi, the media, the whole freaking country loves her. It's like we all grew up with her, you know?"

I nod, recalling all the television shows I watched as a kid that starred Brooke. She's otherworldly gorgeous, with dark, almond shaped eyes, long black hair, and the fullest lips I've ever seen. And they're real. She's the face, technically the mouth, for two or three popular lipstick brands.

"I can't imagine it being more surreal than this. It's wild being here, on set, a part of this experience. I'm still processing." I offer as much of the truth as I can without sounding like an Eli Holt groupie. Fan girl. Whatever.

"Yeah." Harlow nods. "I remember my first film. I couldn't stop staring at everyone."

"It's ridiculous, isn't it?"

"Totally." She flips her chin toward the hotel. "Want to grab dinner? I'm starving."

I stand from the bench we're sitting on, located just off set. "Sure. But honestly, I'm ready for a change of scenery. Tonight's the night we should head into town. One of the crew guys told me about a local spot. Seafood. Want to try it?"

"Absolutely."

"Awesome, let's go."

Harlow and I walk to the front of the hotel and pile into a taxi. I offer the name of the restaurant and within ten minutes, we pull up to an unassuming, brightly colored, music bumping, local restaurant that I'm already a little bit in love with.

It reminds me of simplicity and sincerity and happier times. It reminds me a little bit of home, of Shooters.

Tugging Harlow out of the cab, I grin at her. "First round is on me."

The inside is brimming with fun – loud, boisterous, and

so local it wraps around me like a hug. Harlow and I saunter to the bar.

"Can we order food?" I ask the bartender, who flashes me a grin.

"Of course." He hands me two menus. "Take a seat wherever or keep me company here."

I face Harlow, who wiggles her eyebrows.

We slide onto barstools and scan the menu.

"Have you ladies decided yet?" The bartender appears after a few minutes of pondering the seafood options.

"Yes." Harlow lifts her menu, her index finger on the appetizer section. "We'll take chips and guac."

"The calamari," I add.

"Some clams on the half-shell." Harlow directs her question to me and I flick my fingers, tacking it on to our order.

"And fries."

Harlow grins. "This is the best dinner ever."

The bartender chuckles. "And for drinks?"

"Margarita," I order.

"Make it a pitcher." Harlow swivels her stool back to the bartender. "What's your name, anyway?"

"Laurence."

"I'm Harlow and this is Zoe."

"Nice to meet you." I offer Laurence my hand.

My phone buzzes and I glance at the incoming message.

Hollywood: Hey. Want to meet up and run lines?

My stomach twists as a goofy grin spreads across my face. He's reaching out to me. Stop it. He's only reaching out because he left me hanging, in the middle of a makeout session, on the beach.

Plus, he's about to see his ex-girlfriend and re-enact passionate sex scenes with her. You're here with a friend. Having a girl's night.

My fingers glide over the screen as I debate what to do.

"Come on, girl. We're doing shots. I haven't had a girl's night in a long time." Harlow squeezes my elbow, forcing me to glance up.

The carefree relief that lines her expression causes me to grin back. Dropping my phone back into my purse, I focus on the here and now.

I have no business getting sucked in by a Hollywood heartthrob. Especially one I work for. And definitely not one who can't decide if he's running hot or cold toward me.

"Laurence, we need all the rum," I holler over the bar. He shoots me a wicked grin and nods.

Minutes later, the three of us down a shot of rum.

And there goes the night.

"Shut up! You seriously had to babysit her pet parakeet? That's insane!" I swat Harlow's arm, hysterically laughing at the ridiculousness of some of her previous clients.

"Y'all have no idea. Eli can be a pain in the ass, but he's a gem compared to some of the crazies I've dealt with."

"I bet."

"What about you? You must have had some demanding clients?"

I pop a calamari in my mouth. "Honestly, not like you'd think. I don't really deal with the difficult set; Eli's my most demanding client, and he's pretty chill by Hollywood standards."

"True."

"I mostly train in the MMA circuit. Those guys are just tough. Too tough to look weak and bitch, if you know what I mean."

"Is that how Connor is at the gym?" Harlow asks, fiddling with the hoop in her nose. Her soft drawl wraps around his name and I tip my head, studying her.

Since we've had a few drinks, I decide to just ask her the question I've been wondering about. "How many times have you guys hooked up?"

She groans, face palming herself.

"It's fine. Connor's a great guy."

"He's closed off and infuriating," Harlow mutters, draining her margarita and nodding when Laurence refills it from the pitcher we ordered.

"Most of the guys in the circuit are. You kind of have to be a different sort of breed to take shots to the head for fun."

"I just, I never know where I stand with him."

Sipping my drink, I roll her words over in my mind. "I know what you mean."

"Does he, is he … gah. Does he date?"

I swivel toward her, shaking my head slowly. "I don't know of anyone serious. Fan girls fall all over him, but he doesn't give them the time of day. When he's at the gym, he's locked in. Piece of advice?"

She nods.

"Take things with Connor at face value. He's amazing, but he keeps his cards close to the chest. If you don't want to get hurt, don't read into anything except exactly what he tells you."

Harlow chews her lip. "That makes sense. Piece of advice?"

"Hmm?" I look up, halting the arc the chip is making from the guacamole bowl to my mouth.

"Follow your own advice. With Eli."

I wince, feeling the blush creep up my neck. "You know,

most of the time I can't decide if I even like him. And yet, I really fucking *like* him."

"I know what you mean. It sucks."

"Boys are stupid."

"Let's forget them and dance our asses off."

I hold up my glass, clinking it against hers. In this moment, I miss Charlie. I miss careless fun without the constant worrying.

And now, my worries have only increased with my folded-up paper tucked securely in the side pocket of my suitcase.

How many more pitchers of margaritas will I order?

How many more nights of random dancing will I enjoy?

Harlow's face is flushed, laughter filling the air around her as she nods at whatever Laurence is saying.

Will I ever be that carefree again?

"Y'all. These shots are no joke." Harlow shakes a shot glass, rum sloshing over the side. Her accent thickens with each drink. "Is this even rum?" She sniffs the dark liquid, her face contorting. "I feel like it's gotta be laced with elephant tranquilizers or something serious."

"It's rum." Laurence chuckles, gripping the bottle by its neck and placing it in front of Harlow. "It's just legit rum. Locally produced."

"It's dangerous." Harlow agrees, polishing off her shot and slamming her tiny glass on the flat surface of the bar. "You're up, Zoe. Tonight, we forget about the stupid boys who create nothing but heartache and drink until our heads ache instead."

How many more shots of rum will I take on a whim?

"Pour me one, Laurence." I down a shot, grimacing as it streaks a blaze of fire down my throat, warming my belly.

Now that the sun has set, the music is bumping, and the

crowd is growing. I breathe in the atmosphere of the bar. Bright, colored lights decorate the walls, tables have been pushed from the center of the room to the periphery to make more room for dancing, and a beat pulses through the air.

"I love this music!" I lean closer to Harlow, who slips off her barstool and grabs my hand.

"It's traditional. An African beat with a creole flair. Let's go dance!"

I laugh. "No way can I go out there. I'm an awful dancer!"

Laurence collects our empty shot glasses and wags a finger at me. "Enjoy tonight, mon amie, for tonight is all we have right now."

My brain tumbles over Laurence's words. I'm not sure if it's his words, his tone, or the solemn expression on his face when he says them.

In my tipsy state, Laurence's logic fills me with acceptance. I need to start embracing the moments, not question how many more I have left.

Leaving my purse at the bar like the American tourist I am, I follow Harlow into the crowd and lose myself in the swell of dancing bodies and lively music.

I close my eyes, letting the movement of so many bodies, the deep rumble of the African drums, the perfume of spirits and sweet cocktails, roll over me, pulling me into a tumbling wave of sensation. The lights dance behind my eyelids as I lift my arms in the air, crossing them at the wrists, and rotate my hips in time with the beat.

Female laughter rings out around me as a group of women pull Harlow and me into their dancing circle. Grinning at them, my eyes pop open, and I laugh, giving myself up to this moment.

To freedom. To pleasure.

To the sheer enjoyment of dancing.

The women keep me protected from the leering eyes and handsy hands of random men. The drinks flow freely, the music beats on.

And we drink and dance to the night.

To the moment.

To this incredible experience with strangers who feel like friends.

IT'S LATE when I stumble through the doors of the hotel. The lobby is quiet, the scent of fresh flowers and sea air rolling through the open space like a gentle wave. Harlow's stumbling feet and stuttering words are a constant source of entertainment. I snort as she drapes her arms around my shoulders in a sloppy hug.

"I forgot what it's like to have a girl friend."

"Tonight was fun, Har. I'm glad we're friends."

"I'm relieved." She pats her hand against my cheek, snagging a strand of my hair in her chunky ring.

I wince as she pulls away, but she doesn't notice. "Get to bed, Harlow. You're going to be feeling this tomorrow."

"What about you?" she slurs, her eyes heavy as she glances at me over her shoulder.

"I feel too full to feel tired."

"We ate hours ago," she snickers.

"Too full of energy then."

"I don't know what the fuck you're talking about. I'm going to sleep." Harlow offers me a half-wave as she heads down a corridor toward the elevators that will take her to her hotel room.

Instead of following, I walk through the hotel, down to

the beach. Cool sand tickles my toes as I kick off my sandals. A sweet breeze wraps around my bare legs. My head, bursting with the energy of a night out, laden with pretty alcoholic drinks and cloudy with the sinister thoughts I can't escape, spins.

I dig my heels into the wet sand of water's edge, staring into the endless expanse of sea. The night sky is dark but open, beckoning me to share my secret. To confide in the universe the unknown of my future.

Clenching my hands into fists, the blunt edges of my nails bite the skin of my palms. Throwing back my head, I feel strands of sweaty hair stick to the back of my neck and shoulders. My eyes close and I inhale sea and salt and broken promises. Then, my lips drop open and I roar.

The sound of my anguished cry reverberates through my bones, shaking my limbs and scooping fear from my soul.

The whipping wind eats my shriek, swallowing it into the great expanse where the sea meets the sky. My hurt and fear are stamped out by the vastness of nature. Mother Earth extends a gentle caress and dashes the tears from my eyes, the hurt from my heart.

I scream until my throat is raw and the sound of my blood pumping through my veins is blocked out by the rolling waves.

The sand grows colder under my feet.

The wind grows harsher.

The sea rushes up to meet me, the power of its strength a reassuring comfort.

When my lungs are empty and my body falls slack from all the energy expended, I relish the fatigue that wraps around me like a cloak.

Exhaling in relief, I turn to make my way back to my

room. Exhaustion settles in my limbs, my mind grows quiet, and the comfort of sleep beckons.

But the shadow of a hunched figure, a fallen warrior, leaning over the railing of the penthouse balcony halts my steps.

Eli.

His hands clench the railing, his back hunched, his head bowed. He's shirtless, the sinewy strength of his muscles on full display, rippling with every inhale.

In the dark night, in the quiet of stargazing, his arrogance is gone, his confidence vanished. Instead, a vulnerability clings to him, a loneliness that's deeper than the surface. He pushes off the railing, his eyes rising to the beach. To me.

They slam into me and flicker with a sharpness, a recognition that causes me to freeze, my breath lodging in my throat.

His eyes cut me to my core, seeing past the mask I've perfected, penetrating the depth of my soul where my lies are twisted into half-truths and my truths are broken into lies.

My hand lifts to the center of my chest. I dig the heel of my palm in, reminding my heart to beat, my lungs to breathe.

Eli blinks once, slow and lazy.

Then, he stands to his full height, his body like that of a Greek god, his eyes bleeding a Greek tragedy.

He turns quickly and is gone, swallowed by his massive penthouse, hidden in the depths of fame and fortune and status.

I stand there, staring up at his balcony like a lovestruck teenager, until my body shivers from the cold.

Until my heart remembers to beat again.

12

ELI

"Brooke arrived, so Gray wants to move things around for today." Harlow hands me a sheet of paper with a different scene outline than what I thought we'd be shooting.

I nod, studying the changes, before passing it back to her. "Okay."

"That's it?" she asks skeptically, sounding tired. As if she was expecting me to have some kind of outburst. But before I can probe further, my makeup artist, Michelle, steps in front of me with her brush poised.

"Yeah, it's fine. It's not ideal to anticipate one thing and shift at the last minute but it's part of the job." I shut my eyes as Michelle dusts powder over my face. "Besides, it's Brooke. We have an easy rapport and can read each other alright."

"There is that," Harlow comments, a hint of doubt in her tone.

"Why do you say it like that?"

"It must be weird, working with someone you used to — you know." She hisses the last part since we're not alone.

But I'm rarely ever alone while on set and filming, so it's

not like everyone in this room doesn't know some of the details of my sordid dating history. Or the fact that Brooke and I were a short-lived thing nearly a year ago.

"It's really not with her," I explain, leaning farther back in the chair as Michelle works some kind of gel through my eyebrows. "We ended on good terms, both of us acknowledging it wasn't going to work, and remained friendly. I've seen her out in L.A. and at a few parties since."

"Whatever you say," Harlow appeases me, sounding unconvinced. "I need an Advil." I can hear her rummaging in her purse.

"Not feeling well?"

"The rum on this island is not like the rum back home."

I snort, holding out my hand. "Pass me one too."

"Headache?" She places a small tablet in my hand. I pop it into my mouth and hold my hand out for the bottle of water I know she has waiting. As usual, Harlow is on top of everything.

"Yeah, I didn't sleep well last night."

"Too bad. I slept like the dead. It was waking up that sucked."

I chuckle, sipping on the water and thinking about last night. About the third text message Natalie has sent me in three weeks.

We need to talk.

What could we possibly have to talk about?

After she blind-sided me with her lies when I was nearly twenty-four, and then again at twenty-five by marrying Gray Preston, I should know by now that avoiding Natalie is the best course of action. The last time I saw her, almost two months ago, she was drunk out of her mind, dancing in a club. Trying to get her home safely that night was a nightmare and the hangover she nursed the following morning probably put her out of commission for several days.

All my interactions with Natalie leave me feeling a mixture of disappointment, frustration, and regret. Not regret in the normal sense... no, it's more of a nostalgia. A longing for what was followed by heavy remorse for what she lost. What *we* lost. Being in her presence, breathing in the scent of her perfume that pulls me into our twisted past, and looking into her eyes, eyes I once knew better than my own, always leaves me reeling. With each passing occurrence, my inability to read the situation, to understand her, bothers me more and more.

Since Natalie, I've built my wall so high up, you'd need a helicopter to scale it. No one knows the full truth of what went down between us. No one can comprehend the emotional turmoil she raked me through.

No one can understand how much I still worry about her.

"I'm pregnant." Those words should have signaled a nightmare for a guy like me, in the position I was in back then. Broke, no job prospects, no defined future plans. And yet, all I felt was this undeniable flicker of hope. I was going to be a father. I was going to create a family.

God was giving me an incredible responsibility to become the type of man I always wanted to be. The kind of man who is nothing like my biological father.

I had no idea Natalie was going to terminate the pregnancy, or what that decision would cost me.

Or cost her.

My phone feels heavy in the pocket of my jeans, a reminder that I haven't responded to her message. That I shouldn't have ignored her.

But I did.

After I received her message last night, I texted Zoe

instead. I messaged her to see if she wanted to run lines, and she ignored me.

I wound up pacing the floors of my penthouse like some uptight parent pissed because my kid didn't check in. I hated how worried I was about her. I hated the disturbing thoughts that swirled in my mind of her drinking and dancing and going home with a man who isn't me. The scenarios I concocted in my head left me feeling restless and agitated. Needing air, I stepped onto the balcony, pushing out into the cool night.

And there she was, standing with her feet in the ocean, screaming into the sea.

The anguish on her face twisted my stomach. The pain that consumed her sobs broke something in my chest. I watched her, beautiful and tormented and so goddamn confusing, until her fury turned to acceptance.

That chilling notion frightened me more than not knowing what had caused her so much pain.

I ached for her, wanting to absorb her hurts into my skin and let them mingle with mine.

Jesus.

I scrub a hand over my face, earning a cluck from Michelle. I need to pull my shit together. Zoe should just be another woman on my team, on my payroll. All I should care about is if she shows up to train me like I pay her to.

Instead, her honey eyes seem to follow me during the day and appear in my dreams at night.

"Maybe you can grab a nap after you shoot the first two scenes." Harlow's voice cuts through my thoughts.

"Huh?"

"A nap. You can probably sneak one in around lunchtime."

"Oh, yeah. I'll try to do that. You should too."

"I know. I feel even worse now than I did when I woke up."

Opening my eyes as Michelle steps back, I take a good hard look at Harlow. Her skin is pale, her hair limp, big sunglasses covering her eyes. "You look like crap." I gesture toward her disheveled appearance.

"I don't remember the last time I felt this hungover," she admits, a rare occurrence for my type A, ridiculously organized, annoyingly chipper assistant.

"Everything okay?" I lean forward in my chair, wondering if it's her mom again. Michelle gives me more space as she rummages through her products.

Harlow nods, "How'd your workout go today?"

"I scheduled Zoe for the afternoon."

"For the best," Harlow breathes, uncapping her bottle of water and taking a small sip.

"Why? What's going on?" My suspicion churns like acid in my stomach. Does Harlow know what's wrong with Zoe? Did they go out last night?

Is that why she didn't answer me?

Did something happen to make her scream at the sea, cry tears of helplessness?

"Nothing. I'm recovering." Harlow yawns. "You need me this morning?"

I glare at her, waiting for her to offer some insight about Zoe's whereabouts, but my assistant stays tight-lipped.

I flip my chin at her, recalling my conversation with my publicist this morning. "Actually, I need you for about an hour on set today. Can you take some shots of me and Brooke for my social media platforms? Helen wants to spin shit in a positive way. Apparently, media outlets are speculating about some big blowout of Brooke and I working together." I scoff, hating the media more with each passing year. "So Helen wants to do some posts that show how well we work together, how sincere our friendship really is."

Harlow sighs, disappointed like I knew she would be. But work is work. I can't blow off Helen because Harlow is hungover. "Fine. I'll go grab a camera."

"And a fruit smoothie?" I ask, offering her a smile. "One for you too. It will give you some energy."

The door to the trailer slams behind her.

Sighing, I lean back into my chair and signal for Michelle to continue.

"Eli, God, it's good to see you." Brooke pulls me into a hug.

"Hey Brookie. You too." I wrap my arms around her, pressing a quick kiss to her cheek.

Brooke is *that* girl. The hypnotizingly beautiful one who turns every head in every room she enters. She definitely turned mine the first time I saw her. Now, I'm just happy to see a familiar face and work with a woman committed to her craft. One who won't cause insane levels of drama like several of my past co-stars.

Her chocolate brown eyes crinkle as she smiles back. "We should catch up. I can't believe how long it's been since I've seen you. I think Caroline Reese's surprise fortieth birthday party was the last time?"

I nod, recalling the night fondly. Caroline's husband, Joe, threw quite the party. "She was hysterical."

"Drunk out of her mind. I thought Joe was going to die when she popped out of her own cake."

I tip my head toward the set. "You ready for this?"

"Absolutely. It seems your character is bewitched by mine." She winks.

"Yeah, after your character pretty much seduces mine."

Brooke shrugs, stepping onto the set. "You know how it goes, handsome," she quips over her shoulder. "Want to grab dinner tonight? Catch up?"

"Sure. You can fill me in on the new man in your life."

Her face brightens, her eyes taking on a hint of longing. "I hope he's able to visit while we're filming. You would absolutely adore him. Everyone does."

"Someone's in love," I muse as Brooke blushes. "Achara? 8PM?"

"Perfect." She flags down her assistant and asks for a copy of the script. "We're doing the meet cute first?"

I nod.

She flips through a few pages, whistling under her breath as her eyes flash to mine. "We've got some steamy sex scenes coming up. This one today." She taps a finger against her script before rolling it up and smacking it against my shoulder. "You sure you're up for this?" she teases, knowing how the characters I've played in the past ambled around half-naked for most of the films.

Still, this movie is calling for the most passionate sex scenes I've ever shot.

I laugh, swatting her script away. "Hope you can keep up with me, Brookie."

"Ah, you know that's never been a problem," she jokes back.

A movement behind Brooke catches my eye. A flash of emerald green.

I turn slightly and my gaze slams into Zoe's.

Unprepared to see her on set, I fumble.

Standing to her left, spearing a straw into a large iced coffee, is Harlow.

Zoe's eyes widen in surprise, her bottom lip trapped

between her teeth, worrying itself back and forth. She's dressed in an emerald green pleated skirt that runs like silk to above her ankles and a cropped white halter that ties around her neck, showing off tanned shoulders, and dipping down to offer the barest hint of cleavage.

Instead of the train wreck that is Harlow, Zoe looks incredible. Not at all hungover, no bags shadowing her eyes, no bedhead or grogginess.

There are no signs that she tried to fight Mother Nature singlehandedly last night. No tells that hours ago she was a blubbering mess, swearing at the horizon.

Instead, she looks fucking edible. Her hair hangs around her shoulders, her posture rigid, her eyes clear.

Ignoring her presence — she shouldn't even be here — and the way she rattles my nerves, I turn away.

But not before I notice Brooke's gaze land on Zoe. Touching my arm, she offers me a sympathetic look. "If you care about her, you should prepare her for these scenes."

I shake my head. "It's nothing."

Brooke sighs, her expression softening even though I can read the disappointment in her eyes.

"You guys all set?" Gray asks, stepping into our little huddle and gesturing toward our marks.

"Yeah." I saunter off to my starting point.

Tuning out the noise, I close my eyes and transform into Dr. Henry Shorn.

When Gray calls "action," I am one thousand percent focused on learning to fish as a blind man, with zero fucks given to the arctic blast blowing from Harlow's gaze or the hot fire emanating from Zoe.

"Cut!" Gray calls out when I finish the scene.

"That's a wrap," Brian announces after a quick consultation with Gray. "Okay, since Brooke's here, we're going to move some things around. Take ten. When we return, we're going to jump into Henry's and Adelina's reunion scene."

"That's out of order," I blurt out like an idiot, since most scenes aren't shot in chronological order. Obviously, the reunion scene takes place a hell of a long time after the meet cute.

Brian furrows his eyebrows at me. I glance at the ground, reminding myself how much I suck at being professional whenever Zoe is near.

"I'm just doing a quick touchup in hair and makeup," Brooke says, dashing off to her stylists. Her hair has already been curled, falling down her back like a curtain. Her makeup is perfect, drawing attention to her luscious mouth. Her dress, tight in all the right places, pays homage to her former career as a supermodel.

When I note the crestfallen expression on Zoe's face, I know I'm in trouble. Tucking a strand of violet hair nervously behind her ear, she shuffles uncertainly.

It's cute. It's sincere. It's innocent in a way that tugs at my heart, causing it to expand upward into my throat.

There aren't many women in the world who wouldn't be intimidated by Brooke Silver.

Zoe sticks around, hanging with Harlow, who fiddles with the settings on a fancy camera she managed to swipe from someone on short notice.

Zoe's eyes are trained on set, not quite meeting my gaze but still somehow focused on me.

Nerves churn in my stomach, quickly replaced by anger.

Why am I letting her rattle me? Who cares if she's on set hanging with Harlow? I'm filming the movie of my career. Of course I have a beautiful co-star.

Who does Zoe think she is just showing up, looking like heaven and hell procreated, giving me looks after she spent the night doing god knows what with god knows who? She never even bothered to respond to my message.

Her eyes flash up to mine. The flicker of vulnerability in their butterscotch depths irritates me, replacing my concern for her with frustration. I don't owe her anything. I asked her to hang out, and she blew me off.

I told her I'd only disappoint her. That I don't stick around. I've shown her, even though it nearly killed me, that I won't cross the lines we're blurring, no matter how badly I want to.

I turn away and walk over to my marker.

"Okay." Brooke smiles, sauntering closer to me. "I'm ready."

Brian claps as actors and crew jump into motion. "Places, people. Lights."

"Quiet on set!"

Silence descends over the set like a curtain, blocking out everything outside of this moment.

Right now, the only person I can focus on is Brooke.

Her breath hitches, her eyes widen, and her mouth parts the slightest bit, a sigh falling from her lips. It ripples the air between us, charging it with a natural electricity needed for this scene.

I fight my grin, knowing we're about to make one hell of a movie.

"Action!"

13

ZOE

I'm not insecure. I never have been.

I've always known my place in the world and how to navigate it.

This feeling of a sour stomach coupled with a blaze of heat across the back of my neck, is something new. It surprises me, the intensity of this feeling. Of knowing that in certain areas, I am lacking. I am less-than.

Brooke Silver is a queen.

Long black hair that curls to just above the swell of her ass, dark, almond-shaped eyes that bewitch when they land on you, a perfect nose, upturned the tiniest bit at the end, and a perfectly symmetrical face. For my entire childhood, she was *the* child-star. The one in every kids show, family sitcom, and major Blockbuster. Then, she was *the* supermodel. The one who walked every runway in every European city and graced the covers of all the major magazines.

When that grew old, she returned to her roots, jumping back into feature films as easily as I navigate gym equipment and racks of dumbbells. Effortlessly. Naturally.

But it's not only her looks that cause my heart to ache in my chest. No, that'd be too shallow.

It's the way she moves around Eli, like she knows him intimately, and she does. Not just her body, but her heart. When the director calls "action," the world falls away, and I am entranced by the scene unfolding on set.

The slight uptick of Eli's mouth, uncertain with a shadow of hope until Henry realizes that it is, in fact, his beloved, Adelina. Then, Eli's face transforms. His eyebrows rise, his mouth drops open in surprise, and his hands, they cup Adelina's cheeks, thumbs brushing over her cheekbones, his pinkie trailing down the side of her face and hooking around the back of her neck. He drops his mouth to hers slowly, reverently, desperately.

She arches into him, her hair tipping toward the ground until he fists it in his hand, pulling her flush against his chest.

I can't see her expression, but I can read the wonder in his. The need. The hunger.

His mouth crashes over hers, almost violent in its intensity. She moans, the sound splitting the air until the hairs on my arms stand to attention. I'm drawn to them, like a voyeuristic shadow, desperate for more, and ashamed.

Jealousy churns in my stomach, an unfamiliar sensation of inadequacy.

The kiss on set breaks as Brooke pulls back, her fingers digging into the back of Eli's neck as she whispers, breathless, "Oh, my love. I've prayed for you, for this. For us." Then her lips are fused to his as he lifts her off the ground and walks almost drunkenly until her back slams into a tree trunk. As his hands undress her, hurriedly and desperate, his eyes closed as if he knows her body from muscle memory, and her frantic panting fills the air, I silently snap one photo on my iPhone, turn away, and slip off set.

Back in my room, I study the photo of Eli and Brooke.

Unbridled passion. Yearning lust. Desperate need.

Whatever was between them was more than. Maybe not hearts and rainbows, true love forever, but it was more than a fling, a hook-up, or a "it's just sex" arrangement.

The realization burns way more than it should. Eli kissed me once. Probably from gratitude for helping him with his role. It didn't mean anything to him. If it had, he would have stopped me as I walked away, or reached out with more than a text message asking to rehearse lines.

I was a brief lapse in judgement for him. A random moment that was better fulfilled by kissing than speaking. It didn't mean anything.

I don't mean anything.

Dropping my phone on the bed, I collapse in my desk chair and open my laptop, suddenly desperate to speak with Charlie. I need my friend, someone who can ground me in my real life as I float into this new world like a buoy without an anchor.

Pulling up the FaceTime app, a reminder alert floats in the corner of my screen.

Subject: Reminder - Call Dr. Salinas

Shit, I'm supposed to schedule a breast screening.

Ignoring it, I dial my dad instead. When he doesn't answer, I leave him a voicemail with a reminder to call *his* doctor. Hypocrite much?

Sighing, I press Charlie's contact next.

"Tell me everything about your glamorous life!" Charlie answers, holding the phone on top of the bar at Shooters, the beer taps behind her.

"I miss you!" I smile, a soothing sensation washing over me at the sound of my best friend's voice.

"I miss you too, babe. Sunday Night Football blows without you."

"But the extra pitcher of beer you convinced Dad to do with every order of wings?"

"A hit!" Charlie literally pats herself on the shoulder. "Papa Clark is on the verge of adopting me. We could be sisters for real!"

"How is Dad? I just called him, but he didn't answer."

Charlie's expression sobers and my heart lurches into my throat, my fingers itchy with energy. I just spoke to Dad two days ago and while he was his optimistic and positive self, I could tell from his voice that he was missing me.

"He's okay." Charlie glances away from the screen before inching her face closer and dropping her voice. "Dr. Kent had a cancellation yesterday, so they were able to move his appointment up. Dr. Kent wants him to come back for some additional testing."

Frowning, I feel my nerves zing into heightened panic. "Why?"

"I don't know. He didn't want to talk about it. I even tried to liquor him up. All I know is that he has a follow-up appointment in two weeks. Don't worry, I'm going."

Tears prick the corners of my eyes. I know, in my heart of hearts, that additional testing isn't favorable where Dad's eyesight is concerned. "Is he okay?"

Charlie nods, "He's acting like himself. I mean, obviously, he's missing you, but he's being normal."

Blowing out a deep breath, my cheeks puff out.

Charlie's eyes narrow. "What's going on, Zo?"

"Ahhh." Tears gather in my eyes.

"Homesick?"

I nod.

"That's normal, babe."

"Eli kissed me."

"What?" Charlie shrieks, glancing up from the phone. "No, I'm fine, Fred. Enjoy your fish and chips." Her gaze returns to the screen. "Are you effing *serious*? You better be serious because if you lied about that…wait, why are you crying?"

Dropping my face into my hand, I hide my stupid traitor tears.

"Zoe, what happened?" Charlie gentles her tone, the concern in her voice strong. She gathers her hair into a high ponytail and asks someone to cover the bar for her. I hope it isn't Fred. Moments later, she's sitting on the bathroom countertop, peering at me expectantly.

"He kissed me. We, I don't know, sort of started hooking up on the beach."

"The beach?!"

My shame from the moment when Eli told me to get up, my stomach stuck in the granules of sand, my heart thudding in my chest like a butterfly's wings flapping against a net, rushes to the surface all over again. "And then, he, he abruptly ended it, called me his employee."

She wrinkles her nose. "Ew."

"I know."

"Take a deep breath, Zoe. What happened afterwards?"

"I don't know. I went out for drinks with Harlow. We had a real girl's night, made me miss you."

"Don't replace me, bitch."

"Never."

"And then, Eli messaged me to help him run lines." I click my tongue. "His character deals with blindness so…"

Charlie nods.

"And now, his co-star had to be replaced and Brooke Silver is here."

"Shut the heck up." Charlie's mouth drops open, her blue eyes nearly bugging out of her head.

"You look like an alien."

"I feel like I stepped into an alternate universe. Did you meet the she-god?"

"I'm glad that's your takeaway."

"Wait. Do you *like* Eli Holt?" Charlie asks, horror mixed with delight flashing across her face in a strange expression of furrowed brows and a crazy smile.

I sigh. "I don't know what I'm thinking."

"Holy shit. He really got to you, didn't he? I thought you just liked messing with him and that the whole flirtation between you guys was cute and funny. But not *this*." She shakes her finger at me. "Don't let that man make you cry, boo. No man is worth your tears. Only Papa Clark."

I swipe the back of my hand across my eyes. "What do I do?"

"You train him. Do the job you went to do, focus on the opportunity to expand your business. Don't let Eli Holt distract you from why you're there. You got this, Zoe. You're the most ambitious, badass bitch I know. Don't go acting basic."

I snort at the severity of her tone. "You really are my best friend."

"Duh. Now, tell me about this kiss." She licks her lips, grinning devilishly.

I laugh. "Full details later, I promise. But I actually need to prepare for my training session with Eli."

"Really? I see how it is, Zo."

"Shut it. I'll call you soon. Promise."

"Mean it?"

"Swear it."

"Okay. Love you."

"Love you, too. Thanks, Charlie."

"Bye bae."

I disconnect the call, open the closet, and pull out my suitcase. Unzipping the side pocket, I unfold the white piece of paper with my BRCA results and stare at the large question mark stamped over my future.

I need to schedule the screening.

Should I do preventative surgery?

Positive for BRCA 1 and BRCA 2.

Images of my mom, her head bald, her body frail flicker through my mind.

Then come more recent moments containing my grandma in her final days.

Squeezing my eyes shut, I know this is my fate.

I won't have the fairytale ending that girls like Charlie speak of with certainty. Marriage. Babies. Fulfilling, lifelong careers. Growing old and wrinkly like a raisin, sitting on a rocking chair on a wraparound porch next to the man I built a life with. It's not in the cards for me.

I have this moment. The present. Right now. I have to build my dream career as fast as possible, ensure dad's financial stability, fall in and out of love so I can live that pinnacle of the human experience before I kick the bucket.

Feel all the emotions, do all the things, embrace all the moments.

Squaring my shoulders, I slip the paper on my keyboard and close my laptop.

This is my life. And damn it, I intend to live it.

The chirp of a text message rings out.

Eli: Sorry, need to cancel today's session.

Damn him. He shouldn't blow me off with his career on the line.

Me: Reschedule?

Eli: Get back to you.
Me (to Harlow): Dinner and drinks?
Several minutes pass before Harlow responds.
Harlow: Are you trying to kill me? I'm so hungover.
Me: YOLO.
Harlow: Bish, meet me in the lobby at 9. I'm napping now.

Me: You're the best. Mean it.

14

ELI

"I think I'm going to marry him." Brooke flashes heart eyes as she talks about her boyfriend, Jean Michel.

"And move to Paris?" I snort, her fairytale relationship making me nauseous…and a tad jealous with how effortless it seems.

Aren't real relationships, the ones where marriage is discussed, messy and soul sucking? At least, that's been my experience.

Brooke just laughs, waving a hand at me. "You'll see, Eli. When you meet the right woman, even Paris doesn't seem that farfetched."

"If you say so, Brookie."

"I do. I've been in this industry a lot longer than you. Trust me, finding the right person to share your life with is difficult for everyone. It's even harder for people like us. Months spent filming on location, flying around the world for premieres, engaging in endless interviews." She lifts her linen napkin to dab the corner of her mouth. "There's a lot of pressure on the relationship right from the start. Why do you think so many of us have partners also in the industry?"

I think of my friends from L.A. and their significant others. Brooke's right – nearly all of them are in the Hollywood world. The thought depresses me, making my stomach sink. When I imagine my happily-ever-after, it's in a simple house, with the mess and clutter of children. A whole basketball team of them. Sticky hands and sloppy kisses. A woman whose warmth could heat our entire home.

Not that I would ever admit that out loud, and certainly not to Brooke.

"Jean Michel understands that," she continues, sharing more about Jean Michel's modeling career.

Our conversation drifts to common friends, shared acquaintances, and upcoming movie roles we're considering auditioning for. However, her words stay with me throughout dinner. About finding the right person. About the pressures of our careers. Something about her easy acceptance when she said them, even though I know she spoke the truth, rubbed me the wrong way.

It made the possibility of finding a partner almost hopeless. It made Brooke's relationship with Jean Michel seem unrealistic for the majority of us.

It reaffirmed the belief that I'll always be alone, even though I don't want to be.

I SPOT her the moment I leave Achara. The brightness of her purple hair, the outline of her perfect body, dressed way too sexily for walking around a hotel on a weeknight.

Brooke follows my line of vision and smiles. "She's beautiful, Eli."

"She's my trainer, Brooke."

"If you say so." She chuckles. "Thanks for dinner. I'll see

you tomorrow." She brushes a kiss against my cheek just as Zoe turns in our direction.

As Brooke walks toward the elevator, I keep my gaze trained on Zoe, on the widening of her eyes, the blush creeping across her face. She forces a tight smile and lifts one hand in a half-wave, before turning around and walking through the lobby to the front of the hotel.

Damn it. Where the hell is she going? And who is she going with?

I stride toward the sliding doors leading outside. To where Zoe is probably slipping into a cab, about to head into Victoria. Bursting through the doors, the heat of the tropics hits me full in the face.

"Violet!" I call out. Zoe looks up, a frown on her face. "What's wrong?"

She shakes her phone clutched in her hand. "Harlow had to cancel on me." She gives me the once-over. "Dinner worth skipping out on training?" Her voice is clipped, her features tight.

"You're angry." I frown, reaching for her.

She steps back, her eyes narrowed and her face flushed. "Of course I'm angry, Eli!"

Several people waiting at the taxi stand glance at us curiously. I sigh, tilting my head to a quiet bench off to the side.

Zoe strides toward the bench, not sparing me a second glance to make sure I'm following.

She really is angry, and not because she didn't get something she wanted, *expected* from me, but because she holds me to the same standards as herself.

And I disappointed her.

When she reaches the bench, she whirls around, her index finger pointed between us like a barrier. "You blew off your training session, for *your* film. You know, the one where you're playing a defining role for your career, so you could have dinner with your ex-girlfriend? Are you kidding me?"

"It's more complicated than that," I mutter lamely, not wanting to explain that before dinner, I dealt with a frantic Natalie, desperately trying to get hold of Gray. As usual, I didn't understand her motives, but the fear in her voice indicated that it was important. As usual, I did my best to help her.

"I don't believe you," Zoe murmurs, and the thread of honesty in her voice hurts.

"You don't have to. But I'm telling you the truth. What are you doing now, anyway?"

"Nothing. I was supposed to meet Harlow, grab dinner and drinks. But she's not feeling great."

"She's nursing a wicked hangover." I grip the back of my neck, sitting on the bench.

Zoe sighs, looking out over the expanse of tropical trees and flowers. With each exhale, her eyes travel farther away. "It's beautiful here."

At the ache in her tone I nod, studying her profile. God, she's gorgeous. And real. And exposed in a way I wish I could be.

"Come on." I stand up, holding my hand out like an olive branch. "Let's go get dinner and drinks."

"You just ate."

"Coconut soup and lettuce wraps." I gag. "After today, I need a big, fat, juicy burger with fries. And alcohol. Don't tell my trainer, she's a tyrant."

Zoe stares at me for a beat before a peal of laughter falls from her lips. "Okay, I feel you, Hollywood. Consider this the ultimate cheat day. But tomorrow —"

"I show up, I train, no excuses."

"I don't care how hungover you are."

"What about you?" I point out.

"I can handle my liquor, thank you very much." She takes my offered hand and pulls me toward the taxi stand. "Here. Now. This is my life," she whispers, her fingers squeezing mine.

"This way." She tugs my hand down a side street once we slide out of the cab.

"Who are you? A local?"

She grins at me over her shoulder and my breath lodges in my throat like a brick. It blocks off my oxygen supply, sucking rational thought from my mind. In this moment, with the colorful lights of a nearby restaurant lighting her up, color high on her cheekbones, her hair a wavy mess that tumbles over her shoulder, she's breathtaking. Effortlessly, unassumingly so.

Like the first snowfall of winter.

"Come on!" She pulls me along, into the restaurant with the blinking Christmas lights.

Inside, the walls are a bright yellow, fans turn nonstop from the ceilings, and a boisterous warmth invites us deeper, carrying us right up to the bar.

"*Bonsoir, mon amie.*" The bartender leans over the bar to kiss both her cheeks. My back stiffens, my hand turning rigid in hers.

She squeezes my fingers tighter, chatting and laughing like it's not weird that a bartender would already know her so intimately in the two weeks she's been in the Seychelles.

"Laurence, this is my friend, Eli. Eli, Laurence." She gestures to the bartender, a friendly looking dude with mocha skin and pale green eyes.

"Hey, I know you." He points at me, his smile widening. "You played the elf in that Christmas movie."

I toss my head back and laugh.

He's right. I did play an elf in a Christmas movie. It was the second film I ever did, and one that nearly no one has ever seen. The fact that this is how he recognizes me instantly warms me up to him and his strange relationship with Zoe.

"Yeah, man. Good to meet you." I drop Zoe's hand to shake his and pull out a barstool for her.

Once we're seated, Laurence hunches over the bar, propping up his elbows and dropping his head into his hands. "What kind of a day is it? Shots or fruity cocktails?"

"Fruity cocktails," Zoe replies, running the toe of her flip-flop across the base of the bar. She leans forward, a smile playing over her lips, "I need something bright and fun to drink. Flirty and exciting. With an umbrella, of course."

"I got you, *mon amie*. And for you?"

"Uh, I'll take a Heineken."

Laurence's eyes cut back to Zoe and she snorts, the two of them laughing. Under any other circumstances their bonding would put me on edge, but watching her open up, even with the bartender, and be so carefree hits me with a flicker of happiness.

I like seeing her like this. Relaxed. At ease. Wild waves of violet and black hair caress her shoulders, her sun-kissed skin glows.

She's radiating an energy that's both present and not, eager yet aloof. It's disarming. I wish I could read her thoughts, understand the emotions that flicker across her face like a movie reel.

Laurence raps his knuckles against the top of the bar before pushing back, getting our drinks.

"Hungry?" I ask Zoe.

Her eyes scan the menu. "I can't decide between the curry chicken and the fish."

"Order both."

She glances up, her brow furrowing. "I can't —"

"Laurence," I call out, "let's put in an order for one of every appetizer on the menu. Plus the curry chicken and the fish."

"Okay, you got it," he says.

"Oh my God!" Violet shakes her head, pushing my shoulder. "You can't be serious. That's so wasteful."

"Only if we don't eat it." I swivel on my barstool, my knee tapping her thigh.

"You think we're going to eat —"

"Tonight. Just for tonight, we're not counting calories or worrying about workouts. We're not overthinking and overanalyzing. We're just…here."

"In the now," she breathes, her expression stilling.

"Yeah. In the now." I reach out, my brain no longer connected to my body's movements, and tuck some of her hair behind her shoulder. "You look beautiful, Violet."

She smiles, her cupid's bow dimpling. "Not going to work on me, Hollywood. I'm immune to your lines."

I murmur thanks as Laurence drops a beer in my hand, my eyes never leaving Violet's face. "Keep telling yourself that, babe."

"You're pretty cocky considering your current situation." She swirls a straw around a fruity pink cocktail before fastening her plush lips around the end and taking a sip, her eyes closing.

Jesus Christ. My hand clenches into a fist.

Opening her eyes, Zoe winks.

This girl is going to be the death of me. Never have I met

a woman who loves toying with me the way she does. And never have a I enjoyed being taunted so goddamn much.

"What situation is that, Zoe?" I clink the butt of my bottle against her glass and take a swig of beer, hoping the cool liquid will temper the heat traveling through my veins.

I want to hear her say the words, to stop being coy and call me out on my shit. How messed up is that?

She snickers. "Elephant in the room. Brooke. Silver."

"Ah, yes." I roll my hand over my mouth and chin. "Saw you caught our performance earlier today."

"That was some acting."

"But that's all it was. Acting." I lean forward, my eyes trained on hers.

The air between us crackles to life. Two wills at odd with each other, both desperate to convince the other of our own superiority.

She stares at me for a long beat, the corners of her mouth pinched. "There's a lot of feelings there."

"Of friendship," I grit out, my voice controlled, my fist clenching tighter.

"Friendship," she repeats.

"Food's up," Laurence announces, placing an assortment of plates in front of us.

Zoe blinks, the solemnity of her expression falling away as her easygoing grin slips back into place. Popping a piece of fried calamari in her mouth, she groans in pleasure and my body tightens.

Jesus.

"To tonight." She faces me. "The now."

"The now," I echo, my eyes raking over her face. Flushed cheeks, bright eyes. Caught up in the night.

Something about her expression, the slight sheen of sweat

that beads at her hairline, irks me. Zoe is nothing if not professional, ambitious, determined.

In fact, her training circuits and commitment to her business have been incredibly impressive.

What would make her blow off steam two nights in a row to drink sugary beverages and eat her weight in seafood? What would make her even hint at crossing the professional line between us?

I drain my beer. What the hell is wrong with me?

She's your trainer.

Yeah, keep telling yourself that.

To date, Zoe's done a hell of a better job fighting the attraction between us. And I know if she gives me the slightest indication that she's willing to blur our trainer-client line, I'll give into the temptation in a heartbeat.

The truth is, I wanna roll around in this girl's bed and bring her to the brink of a "come to Jesus" moment.

Not play Freud to the dark corners of her mind.

She wants to get fucked up tonight? I'm willing to play my part.

"Laurence, pour us some shots!" she calls out, her skin flushed, her voice high.

"You got it, *mon amie*."

She leans forward, the soft skin of her lower back itching to be touched. I place a palm along the small of her back, skin to skin. Instead of jerking away, she sways slightly and I curl my hand, my nails grazing her skin.

"Careful, Hollywood, don't want to give a girl ideas."

"I'm going to fill your head with them, Violet."

She turns, her chin dipping into her shoulder, smoldering bedroom eyes like melting caramel. "Promise?" Her voice is taunting, a thread of a dare that I want to say yes to.

Laurence drops off the shots, and Violet hands me one.

"Every. Damn. Thing. Zoe." Her eyes hold mine prisoner, a desperation I don't understand edging her irises.

"And then some," she swears, throwing back the shot and smacking her lips.

"And then some," I repeat, nodding toward the food. "Now eat."

Zoe picks at fried calamari and doctors up the clams on the half shell the way she likes – lemon, horseradish, extra hot sauce.

"Extra spicy, huh?"

"I like the experience more than the ending," she explains, speaking in riddles.

"Not following you, babe. But I'm willing to try it your way." I swipe a clam and nearly put myself into cardiac arrest, coughing.

Zoe laughs, pushing napkins into my hand and holding a glass of water beneath my lips. "Drink this, Hollywood. Can't have you hocking up a lung on my watch."

I swallow long sips of water, my eyes smarting with tears, my throat burning. "Jesus Christ, Violet, you don't mess around."

"No, I don't."

Motioning to Laurence for another beer, I switch to French fries.

"Let's play a game," Zoe suggests, chewing the corner of her mouth.

"What kind of game?"

"Get your head out the gutter."

"You're the one who walks around with blindfolds."

"Sleep masks!"

Chuckling, I hold up a hand in surrender. "What's the game?"

"Two truths and a lie."

"How do you play?" I wipe my mouth with a napkin, noting how she tracks the movement, her mouth parting slightly.

My blood hums with awareness, with want. But Violet keeps her cool, makes me work for it.

It's been so damn long since any girl gave me any type of chase, I'm nearly salivating for the chance to prove just how hard I can fuck her world.

"We each say three things. Two truths. One lie. And the other person has to guess which one is the lie."

"You're cute, Violet. If you wanted to get to know me so badly —"

"I'll start," she cuts me off.

"Alright." I kick my feet up on the rung of her barstool and lean back. "Let me hear it."

"I love horror films. I hate waking up early. I have an older brother."

"You hate waking up early is the lie," I smirk, knowing she's up at 5AM every morning for work.

"Ehhh." Zoe sounds like a buzzer. "I really do hate waking up early. The lie is that I have a brother."

"Wait. You seriously love horror films?"

She grins, contorting her face to look evil.

"You're bizarre," I snort, throwing a fry at her face.

She picks it up and pops it into her mouth. "You have no clue. Your turn."

"Okay. Let's see. I'm a billionaire. Surfing is my favorite hobby. I want to have a basketball team of kids."

"Hm." Zoe frowns, narrowing her gaze and peering from one of my eyes to the next.

"Why so serious?"

"I'm trying to deduce if the billionaire or kids is your lie."

I laugh. "And?"

"Kids. No man wants that many kids."

"Ehhh." I make her buzzer sound and she winces, her eyes dropping to the floor for a moment. "Wrong, babe. I do want a ton of kids. And I really am a billionaire."

"Wait, so surfing is your lie?"

"Yeah. Basketball is my favorite hobby."

"You're really a billionaire?" she murmurs after a beat, some of her enthusiasm deflated.

"My dad, not Derek who raised me and who I love like a father, but my biological one, left me and Evan a shit-ton of money when he died. Companies and properties and trusts. The fucker missed our entire lives. He never gave a damn about us, never sent child support or even tried to communicate with us. He left my mom all on her own, working two jobs and every side hustle imaginable just to make ends meet until she met Derek. And then he kicks the bucket and changes my world overnight about two years ago."

"Damn." Zoe whispers, studying me. "That sucks, Eli. I'm sorry."

I nod, turning back to my beer and taking a gulp. Why the hell did I bring up Dad? I never talk about him. "Don't be sorry, babe. I'm fucking flush, remember?"

She winces, as if I've hurt her. Maybe I have. But Zoe is tearing down too many walls, getting too close to my real thoughts. The ones that rarely make it out of my mouth. "Your turn."

"I want to see the Eiffel Tower at night while eating macarons. I wish I was brave. I hate the color orange."

"You hate the color orange."

She shakes her head. "I wish I was brave."

"Huh?" I grip her thighs and physically shift her body closer to mine. Beneath my touch, her skin is hot, even through the flimsy material of her skirt. "You are brave, babe."

"No, I'm not." She says the words clearly, without judgement.

"Yeah, you are. Not everyone would leave their lives behind to take a job like this."

"Uh, yeah. Pretty much everyone would."

"Nah. You've got balls, Violet. Big, donkey balls."

She snorts, "You're ridiculous."

Laurence drops off more shots.

"You're perfect." I tilt my shot glass of rum toward her until she laughs. Then I throw it back, enjoying how with each drink, the colors burn brighter, the restaurant grows louder, and Zoe looks more and more like a dream just out of my grasp.

She's the unattainable. The goddamn elusive truth wrapped up in so many tangled lies.

"One more." I whisper, returning my hands to her thighs and bracing my weight.

She wraps her hands around my wrists, leaning forward. We're now inches apart. So close that I can count the freckles that decorate the bridge of her nose like sprinkles.

She smells so damn good, like wind and sea and woman.

"Tell me," she whispers, her breath fanning across my lips, sweet like her pink fruity cocktails.

"I'm going to kiss you now. I'm going to fuck you tonight. And tomorrow, you're going to beg for me to do it again."

One side of her mouth ticks, not a smile nor a frown. "Lies. All lies."

"Nah, baby. Every one of those was the fucking truth." I grin, my gaze dropping to her lips before I cover her mouth with mine.

Her mouth is perfectly shaped, warm and willing as I mold my lips to hers. It's heady, the feeling of her mouth moving against mine. Sensual, which is ridiculous because the act is so damn innocent.

Her mouth parts and I dip my tongue inside, languidly. As if we're not making out in front of an entire restaurant full of people.

As if I'm not famous.

And she's not the most confusing woman I've ever met.

I slide my hands up, up, up, skimming her ribcage, her shoulders, until I palm her cheeks. Pulling away, I grin down at her. "Let's get out of here, Violet."

She snorts, but the sound is too breathy, her eyes too hazy with lust to be haughty. "So you can fuck me?"

"Every. Damn. Thing. Promised you, Violet. Mean to keep it." I throw down a wad of cash on the bar and tug Zoe off her barstool.

She follows me out of the colorful restaurant into the quiet night. I pull her toward the main road where we can grab a taxi, but she pulls on my hand, causing me to follow her down an alley instead. She places her back against the wall and glances up at me, a challenge sparking in her eyes.

Moonlight shines off her cheekbones as she bites her lower lip. Her eyelids are heavy with need, her eyes bright with desire.

My heart thumps in my chest, excited and wary at the same time. I want nothing more than to straddle her thighs, cage her in with my arms, and kiss her senseless. But something about the expression on her face, needy yet remote, gives me pause. Connor said Zoe is a thousand percent focused on her business, a woman who walks the straight and narrow. Right now, his words don't add up to the deliriously beautiful, somewhat tipsy, borderline reckless woman standing before me.

"Why are you doing this, Zoe?" I murmur, my thumbs brushing her cheekbones, my hands cupping her cheeks. I angle her head, trying to see into her convoluted mind, to uncover her buried secrets.

"Because I can," she whispers, her breath rippling over my chin, her hands finding the belt loops of my jeans.

"What do you want?" I drop my face a millimeter closer to hers.

"All your lies."

"I have enough to fill every cell in your body."

"Give them to me," she demands, her breasts brushing against my abdomen.

"Two truths and a lie," I remind her. Her hands settle on my hips, the tips of her pinky fingers slipping under my T-shirt and grazing my bare skin. I shiver at her touch. "You're the most unattainable woman I've ever met. This means nothing. I don't trust you."

"You shouldn't." She lifts up onto her tippy toes, placing open-mouthed kisses along my jawline.

"Shouldn't what?"

"Trust me." She pulls back, her eyes completely sober. "I'm the biggest liar there is." She pops the button on my jeans and I stop caring about this game, this conversation, the fact that we're out in the open and I'm about to fuck her against an alley wall.

Instead, I take her advice and focus on the goddamn now.

15

ZOE

His mouth closes over mine with intent, possessive and unyielding. It's only after I part my lips that his fingertips ease their bruising grip on my hips and he slows the pace of his tongue from a crescendo to a melody.

Slow and languid, unhurried and unbothered by all the people who could be watching us right now, we commence making out like two horny teenagers too desperate to seek shelter. A passerby would take one look at us and know the truth — our bodies are a hell of a lot more telling than our words.

We like each other more than we let on. We like each other too much.

Eli rolls his forehead across mine. "You're fucking killing me," he groans, his right hand trailing up from my hip, palming my stomach, until it's pressed against my heaving chest, nestled in the valley of my breasts. "I don't know how to do this with you, Violet."

"Do what?" I breathe out, my body coiled so tightly in anticipation, in desire, in need, it's shaking.

I am shaking.

His hand continues its path, stopping at the base of my throat, his fingers curling around my neck in a motion that shouldn't be provocative yet elicits a whimper from my lips.

"This. Now." He presses a kiss to the underside of my jaw. "And then see you tomorrow to work out."

I swallow, dropping my head back against the concrete wall to give him more access, all the while cursing at myself.

I shouldn't be doing this. He's my employer. If his performance today held an ounce of truth, he's still hung up on Brooke Silver.

Brooke freaking Silver.

"It's different with you," he whispers so low, I strain to make out the words.

But, the words!

They're exactly what I want to hear. What every woman wants to hear, especially in a moment of doubt. The flicker of uncertainty swaying in my stomach is snuffed out.

Closing my eyes, I drape my arms over Eli's shoulders and press up onto my tiptoes. He understands my intent and guides me up the wall until my legs are wrapped around his hips, his erection pressing into my lower abdomen.

The motion is natural, as if he could read my mind. That's the thing with Eli – we push each other's buttons and try to maintain distance, but this part, the chemistry, the physicality, the yearning need, it pulls us together with a force stronger than our combined resolve.

Gone is the clashing of wills. The lashing of tongues. The desperate edge to conquer, the fear of surrender. In its place is a quiet acceptance of what we both know to be true — neither one of us is going to stop this.

So here, in this alley in the center of Victoria, I let Eli Holt fuck me into oblivion.

His hips pin me to the wall, one hand gripping my ass, the other splayed wide next to my head. His eyes are molten, a blazing green flame. Hot enough to burn, hot enough to soothe.

"Why are you doing this, Violet?" he repeats, his voice low and gravelly. The veins in his forearm pop next to my head. I can see the physical restraint he's exercising to keep this conversation going when we should be naked and pressed into each other by now.

What the hell is wrong with this guy?

"Jesus, Hollywood. Come on." I grip his shoulders, my eyes nearly rolling back in their sockets when his erection brushes against my core.

"Answer the question, babe."

"Because I want this. I want this with you. Are you happy?" My eyes jump open, irritated that he's ruining this moment, the one I'm desperate to drown in, with his stupid chatter.

"Tell me, Zoe. Why? I've tried the girl-next-door hometown sweetheart. I also did the unrivaled, sexy temptress who could make a dildo explode. And every woman in between. You know what? They all suck dick the same way. On their knees. But you, babe…" he pauses, a silent fury rippling over his expression.

My head taps back against the cold wall. I hate that I'm wondering if Brooke Silver is the sexy dildo-exploding temptress he mentioned. "I'm what?"

"You're more dangerous than all of them combined. So tell me, why?"

"Two truths and a lie."

He drops his head, biting into the ball of my shoulder in confirmation.

"I want to feel something that has the power to ruin me. I

want an orgasm that rips me wide open. I don't want to *belong* to anyone."

He lifts his head, so achingly slow, my body clenches with anticipation for his expression, a desperate need to see what he's thinking, since he's sure as hell not going to tell me.

His hand slides along the wall, scraping like sandpaper, until it slips behind my neck, squeezing lightly. He studies me, his gaze intent, his face hard. Like a bitter god, impassioned and indignant.

The pressure at the base of my neck intensifies as his fingers squeeze harder.

He licks his bottom lip, a flicker of indecision. "That's three truths, babe."

"No." I shake my head. "I —"

But his mouth closes over mine before I can say the words, his lips bruising in their demand, nurturing in their need.

Eli kisses me so hard that black ink with all the words I can't say uncurl along my skin, like a palimpsest, hovering between blood and flesh, between black lies and even blacker truths.

16

ELI

It was how I always imagined it would be.
Her.

Hot. Intense. Fucking desperate. Pushed up against a wall in a back alley, her tits on full display, bouncing each time I plow into her.

She rained swear words down upon my head, her fingers gripping my neck, her mouth buried in my hair. Around my waist, her thighs clenched and quivered, so goddamn close to release, I could feel it. Feel it in the tightening of my balls, in the frantic pace I set.

And it was nothing like how I imagined it.

Because in the frenzy of fucking, wild eyes, parted lips, nipping teeth, a gentleness emerged.

We're both breathing heavily, our hands tracking each other's movements, our eyes locked on each other's expressions. Stepping back between her parted thighs, I palm her ass, kneading one cheek and then the other, becoming lost in the sounds of her moans all over again. Her eyelids at half-mast, hooded with a lust so thick it moves through my bloodstream like molasses.

Slow and lazy. Languid and sweet.

Golden eyes, the color of autumn leaves just before they fall from the tree, meet mine with an acceptance that breathes life into the vulnerability we're both showing. She wants me again. This. Now. Repeat.

I've wanted her from that first encounter. I've fought it, and cursed it, and pushed her away. And here we are, in a back street in the goddamn Seychelles, about to connect on a level deeper than just sex. More than what we just did.

"Eli," she whimpers, her thighs squeezing my hips. "Please, I need you."

You.

Not "this."

I need *you*.

"I got you, baby." I press kisses to each of her eyelids. With one hand on her ass, her back anchored against the wall, I slide my other hand between us, slipping up her skirt once more. I've already torn her panties and I glimpse the scrap of lace, crumpled on the ground. But this time, I'm in no hurry. This time, I want to savor the moment. The second my fingers glide against her slick folds, she whimpers and I swear.

Silky smooth and so fucking wet, I push two fingers inside her, high on the expression that crosses her face.

Trust.

Her eyes flutter closed, her head rocking against the wall as I slide my fingers in and out, the pad of my thumb tracing tiny, light, barely there circles over her clit.

And fuck, she's so goddamn responsive that my skin heats, my nerve endings exploding. Burning for her, my breathing is labored just watching her face. I feel like a teenage kid all over again, overeager and unsteady.

"Eli, please." She bites the corner of her mouth, her fingertips digging into the flesh of my back, sliding underneath my collar and scoring my skin. "Please."

"Be patient, Violet. I need this as much as you do," I admit, relishing the need that ripples over her features. We already had the release, but now she needs to be taken care of.

For the first time in forever, I want to take care of a woman like she's mine. Not just for the night, but for real.

I don't slow my movements. The moment her breathing pitches higher, a growl rips from my lungs. Sinking to my knees, I hook her legs over my shoulders and bury my face in her center, replacing my fingers with my tongue.

"Oh God." She jerks from the contact, her ass slapping against the concrete before sagging in the space between us. My hands grasp her upper thighs while I lick a smooth line down her core, enjoying every single moan that falls from her mouth. Slow, leisurely strokes that raise her higher in the smallest increments of pleasure.

While she writhes around me, her thighs pressing into my neck in need of relief, I use the tip of my tongue to circle her clit, once, twice. I then unleash my need to have her, consume her, by fucking her with my mouth.

"Eli, Eli, oh God, fuck, baby, please." Words fall from her lips, her hands gripping my hair. "I'm coming," she gasps as I squeeze her thighs, catching her body's tremors with my mouth until she falls still.

"Ready for round two, Violet?" I offer her a devilish grin as I stand to my feet, reach into my pocket for my wallet, pull out a second condom and roll it on. My dick is already hard as a fucking rock, painful in its need to get back inside of this bewildering woman.

She nods, her eyes still hooded, brown hues speckling butterscotch. "Yes."

Lining myself up at her entrance, I push inside again. This time, she quivers around me instantly, and I feel it. Deep in my chest. A connection I haven't experienced since Natalie. "Jesus."

"Jeez Louise." Zoe's hands lace behind my neck as I pause, giving her a second to adjust to me.

I pull all the way back before pushing in again, not stopping until I'm root deep.

She sucks in a breath, her elbows hooking over my shoulders as she draws me into her chest. "Eli." It's a curse laced with wonder. My body jolts from her tone, wishing I could be the man in her life to always cause such marvel.

But knowing I can't be, a part of me never wants to hear it again.

Setting the pace, I block out the warmth of her touch, the caress of her fingers, the smooth feel of her skin gliding over mine.

I work her over until she's screaming my name and I'm growling hers, spilling into her so hard my vision blurs. Dropping my forehead, I try to regulate my breathing, my heart galloping in my chest.

And not only because that was intense, but because my stupid organ already knows I'm in over my head.

"Wow." She squirms, her hips probably aching from being pressed into concrete for god knows how long.

"Yeah," I agree, slipping out of her and returning her to her feet.

My entire being is on edge, brimming with feelings and emotions and so much goddamn messiness, I wish I could be empty once more.

It's late when Zoe and I stumble back into her room.

Small, compact, and tidy, the space makes me frown. I should have her moved to a bigger accommodation.

She's laughing, the glow from earlier wrapping around her like a hug. Carefree and confident, Zoe slips out of her skirt, kicking it to a corner before backpedaling to her bed.

"What're you doing, babe?" I reach behind my neck to yank off my shirt, checking to make sure the door is closed and the lock latched. Last thing I need are goddamn photos of me fucking Zoe circulating on *Gossip*.

Especially considering there's a greater threat of that happening from our back-alley bang than right now.

The backs of her knees hit the bed and she flops backwards, bracing herself on her elbows to watch me undress. "Night's not over, Hollywood."

"Good. Because tomorrow's going to be hell."

She shrugs. "Tomorrow will be one more day."

Frowning, I throw my balled-up shirt at her and walk to her bed. Splayed out beneath me, her white halter top pulled tight across her chest, I grab one end of the tie and pull, until her shirt collapses and her breasts pop free. "You sound dejected, babe. I'll give it to you again tomorrow if you ask nicely."

She snorts. "One night only. The now. Remember, Hollywood?"

Crawling over her, I dip my head and suck her breast into my mouth, clamping down on her nipple until she hisses. Easing off, I glance up and shake my head. "Not a chance in hell, babe."

"Eli."

"I'm going to fuck you for the rest of our time in the

Seychelles. I will give you all the orgasms to rip you wide open. I won't ever make you mine." I say the words, two truths and a lie, before gripping Zoe's hip and sliding into her to fill her up with half-truths and convoluted lies.

Deep down, the greatest lie is the one I tell myself.

17
ZOE

"Morning, babe." He smiles down at me as he walks out of my bathroom, a towel around his waist. Fresh from the shower, drops of water cling to the hard planes of his chest and abdomen and drip from the stubble coating his chin.

"You look like a commercial." I swing my legs to the side of the bed and stand. A wave of dizziness washes over me and I reach out, gripping the end table to keep from falling.

"Thought you could handle your liquor," he shoots back, that stupid grin still in place. Stupid because that mouth is too good to belong to any man. The things he can do with it are criminal.

"Maybe my light headedness is from other pursuits." I turn and smile, ignoring the throb behind my eyelids, the dryness of my mouth.

You're hungover. You're sated. You're a confident woman engaging in hot sex with an unattainable man.

I'll never make you mine.

I shake my head to clear Eli's words from my mind. They're what I wanted to hear, right?

Wrong.

Just one look at him forces me to admit that while I used to relish casual, no-strings-attached-sex, I suck at one night only with him. Yes, I'm living in the moment. Carpe diem, blah, blah. But those eyes on that face with that voice makes my heart twirl like Anna Pavlova in *The Dying Swan*. Plus, the fact that he's still here, chatting me up and grinning like he has nowhere else to be, makes me want things I shouldn't.

Like, him. For more than one night.

Shoving my feet into the slippers housekeeping left at the side of my bed, I stalk to the bathroom, closing the door in Eli's surprised and irritating face.

I stare at myself in the mirror, drawing in deep breaths and trying to rein in the thoughts ricocheting like pinballs around my head. Tears burn behind my eyes and flood my senses.

What is wrong with me?

I had the best damn sex with the hottest guy I ever met last night.

Yeah, last night. And now it's tomorrow. The dreaded "day after."

Dropping my head into my hand, I pinch the bridge of my nose until it hurts, a distraction from my stupid tears.

You're not a crybaby. You accept reality. You're *strong*.

I drop my hand and glance up at my flushed cheeks, messy hair, and lean, naked body.

You're fucked, that's what you are. Fucked in the head for thinking you could do this with a man like Eli Holt.

"Hey. You okay?" Eli calls through the door.

Ugh. Rolling my eyes, I ignore the edge of concern in his tone and flip on the faucet, throwing myself into a hot shower.

Once I feel somewhat human again and open the door to

my bedroom, Hollywood is sitting at my desk, watching a YouTube video.

My heart lodges in my throat as I see the white paper, the bane of my existence, lying face down on my desk.

Did he read it? Does he know?

"This guy is such an asshole. Funny though." He chuckles, glancing up and pointing to the screen where some guys dare each other to drink some type of hemorrhoid inducing hot sauce from shot glasses.

I force a smile, but it feels like plastic on my face.

No, he doesn't know. He would say something.

Wouldn't he?

He stands from the chair and wraps his arms around me. "You okay, babe?"

I breathe in the scent of soap clinging to his skin and center myself.

I did the now. It was amazing. Now, it's a new day.

"I'm fine. I gotta get ready for our session and run some errands."

"Yeah, a reminder kept popping up on your computer. Call your doctor?" He frowns.

I wave a hand, relieved he can't see my face. "It's for my dad."

"Figured as much," he says easily. "You wanna grab breakfast?"

Is he serious? Can he really be so casual after last night? He had his way with me in a skeevy alleyway. In public. And I liked it. More than liked it. Now, he wants to grab poached eggs?

"Nah, I'm fine." I step out of his embrace, gesturing to my towel. "Going to get dressed. See you at 2PM for our workout?"

He nods, his expression solemn before he swipes his

phone and wallet from the dresser. "I'm going to bring my best, Violet."

"I'm going to punish your ass, Holt," I quip, cringing when I hear how the words sound.

Eli laughs, shaking his head on the way to the door, "Is that a promise, babe?"

"Goodbye, Eli. And thanks for last night."

"Trust me, the pleasure was all mine, baby." He caresses my cheek, tucking strands of wet hair behind my shoulder. His grin is lopsided and cute and boyish, causing my heart to stutter. Then he shuts the door behind him and I collapse into my bed.

Baby.

It's the first time he's said it, not counting during sex, and it didn't sound like a cheap shot.

My heart gallops in my chest as I try to regulate my breathing.

Holy fuck. I slept with Eli Holt. Like, slept, slept. In the same bed. For the whole night.

Picking up my phone, I roll my eyes at the stupid reminder to call Dr. Salinas and, vowing to do it later, I FaceTime Charlie instead.

She answers on the first ring, her blond hair piled messily on top of her head. "Soul sister, I've been thinkin' of ya."

"I miss you, Charlie. Why're you in such a good mood?"

"I'm always in a good mood."

"Nope. Something's up with you."

"I could say the same thing to you. You look…normal."

"Normal?" I scoff, sliding back into my twisted sheets and leaning against the headboard.

"Yeah. Like your mind isn't racing a million miles a minute with a to-do list longer than the Octomom's."

"I had sex last night."

"Eli?" My best friend breathes out, her eyes so wide she looks like an alien.

"Eli."

"Holy fucking hell. Are you serious right now? Jesus, Zo, that's like, wow. Tell me everything."

"No way!"

"Damn, he's that good?"

"The best I ever had."

"I'd fall over in shock, but since I know you've been with like five people, I don't feel that's an adequate comparison. Give me more."

I hold up three fingers and Charlie cheers like I just announced my candidacy for political office. "Now, I'm jealous. Wait, wait, how drunk were you?" Charlie closes one eye, peering at me like she's trying to read my mind.

"Not drunk enough."

Her mouth drops open and she leans closer to the screen until I can count the freckles that dust her nose. "Shit, Zoe. You like him."

Tears spring to the corners of my eyes, and the back of my throat burns with all the words I can't say. All the lies I harbor there. "I like him."

"That's amazing!" Charlie whoops, literally twirling around until I feel like I may get motion sickness from the way the screen keeps flipping my image.

"Charlie, I can't, I mean, nothing can happen."

"Why not?"

"He's Hollywood."

"So? Jesus, girl, never knew you needed to be propped up with compliments but —"

"I don't."

"Then, what gives? I'd be trying to wrestle a ring out of any man who could give me three orgasms in one go."

I swipe a hand over my face. "I just, I don't know how to do commitments and there's distance and…"

"You're scared."

I wince at the truth that shines from Charlie's eyes. She's always read me easier than other people. In this moment, with her narrowed eyes, the ends of her hair clamped between her teeth, I know she's turning over ideas in her head.

Ideas I'm not ready to lend any validity to.

"You're not dying, Zoe," she murmurs finally, her tone soft, like she's talking to a child.

Ice rattles through my veins, causing my skin to break out in a sheet of goosebumps. My fingers tremble, making the phone shake, and my face freezes as my mind fogs over.

I open my mouth and close it several times, no words coming out. Staring at Charlie's serious expression, the compassion burning in her blue eyes, I suddenly feel tired. Exhausted. Too drained to deny the truth. Too weak to form another lie.

"You took the test," she says suddenly, her words lashing at me like an accusation even though her expression is pure empathy.

Clearing my throat, my eyes swell with tears and my face crumples like a tissue.

"Shit, Zoe. Why didn't you tell me, babe? What'd it say?"

"Positive."

"BRCA 1 or 2?"

I lift my hand to my face and sob into my own skin.

Charlie's quiet, the sound of her breathing a reminder that I'm not alone. If I'm going to tell anyone, it should be her, right? She's my best friend, someone who's always been in my corner. Someone who can help keep my secret. The person who held me up when Dad started going blind, when Mom passed, when Grandma slipped away.

"Both," I stutter, looking up to see the shock that washes over her face and stays there. Frozen.

"No way." Her voice is hard, but her own eyes are suddenly too large, swimming with unshed tears. "Zo."

"I can't, I don't know how to —"

"You're not dying, babe."

"You don't know that."

Charlie sighs, chewing on her hair like straw. Finally, she shakes her head, throwing up a vehement hand. "Fine, let's pretend you are dying. Does that mean you shouldn't want to experience every single thing that life has to offer? Jesus, Zoe, if this test doesn't prove that life is fragile and you should appreciate every second, every opportunity, than I don't know what does. So let Eli Holt give you enough orgasms to drown in."

I snort, the sound harsh, and we both smile tentatively. "I like him."

"Then like him."

"But, I don't know how to not hurt him."

"Tell him. Tell him the truth."

"No. Everyone here will look at me like, like how people used to look at Dad after his diagnosis. Except I'll be able to see all their pity. I don't want it."

Charlie sighs, nodding her consent. "What do you want, Zo? More than anything, what do you want?"

"To be happy."

Charlie grins, dropping her hair. "Then do that. Every day, do something that brings you happiness. You don't owe explanations to anyone. Do *you*, babe."

"It's not that easy."

"Except it is. It really is. I wish I was with you right now. I'd hug you so hard for not telling me, I may strangle you."

Laughing, I wipe my tears. "I'm sorry."

"Don't be. Be happy. Your dad?"

I shake my head.

"You're going to have to tell him, Zoe."

"Not yet."

"Go have your island adventure. The test results, they're not a death sentence, Zo. They're a warning. To be observant, to keep your appointments, to take care of yourself."

"Charlie, my mom and grandma —"

"Aren't you. So don't go comparing yourself to anyone."

I cast a glance at the clock. "I gotta go."

"Call me later?"

"Duh. I need you to tell me everything going on in your life."

"Yeah, well, at the moment, that's kind of a lot. I love you, Zoe. Too much to let you slip away from fear."

"Love you, Charlie." I grin. "Talk to you later."

"I'll be drunk trying to process the bomb you just dropped on me."

I point a scolding finger at her. "Make sure you don't drive."

"Nah, I'll make Evan or someone give me a ride. Just … call me."

"Evan? Eli's brother?"

Charlie shrugs, the faintest shade of pink blooming in her cheeks. "He's been hanging out at Shooters more and…well, he's better company than Fred."

I laugh. "Fair. Is he the 'kind of a lot' happening in your life right now?"

"Kind of."

"We need to chat."

"We will. I promise."

"Okay. I'll talk to you later." Disconnecting the call, I flop back against my pillows and close my eyes.

I feel lighter after confiding in Charlie. Like now that I'm not the only person carrying around the weight of my secret, there's more room to feel things other than guilt.

Stretching, my body aches deliciously from last night's activities.

Charlie's right. I don't owe anyone anything. I should be happy. I should dive into the things I love. I should take care of myself.

Starting with an amazing workout with Eli Holt.

And followed by orgasms. Of the multiple variety.

18

ELI

"Jesus Christ, Violet, you wanna give me a heart attack?" I snap my towel against Zoe's ass as she sashays onto the beach, clad in the tightest black yoga pants I've ever seen, cutouts running the length of her long legs. Her stomach is bare, a tight crop top accentuating her breasts.

"I'm gonna make you work for it, Hollywood," she quips, a grin touching her lips.

Those lips. Images of them tracking down my abdomen, closing over my dick, flickers through my mind like a goddamn flipagram. I bite the inside of my cheek to keep from groaning.

"For the sweat or for you?"

"Both." She stops in front of me, trailing her fingertips up my abdomen.

My muscles contract at her touch. She smiles, her eyes knowing. "We're gonna go hard today."

"Bring it, baby." I laugh, enjoying her sass.

"I will." She tilts her head to the side. A flicker of unease colors her eyes and she bites her lower lip. "Hollywood, about last night —"

"Nope."

"What do you mean, nope?"

"Not doing this, babe. Last night was amazing. And, it was fun. I like amazing and fun. You?"

Zoe nods, her nose wrinkling as she shades her eyes from the sun. "I do. But —"

"Don't overthink this, Violet. You and me, we can have some fun together and take things as they come. Feel me?"

She glances down at the toe of her sneaker, digging a trail in the sand. "Yeah, I feel you," she finally says.

When she drops into a stretch and the round globes of her ass meet my line of sight, my flippant comments die in my throat, and a growl escapes instead. Zoe's more than just good-time fun. Deep down I know that, or I wouldn't crave her the way I do. Last night was supposed to be a one-off. I was supposed to purge her from my system. Now, instead of focusing on the circuit exercises she's explaining, I'm wondering how I can get her into my bed tonight.

Zoe looks at me over her shoulder, her black and violet hair in a messy braid hanging down her back, taunting me to grip it, wrap it around my wrist, and take her from behind.

"Care to join me, Hollywood?" She nods toward the first station.

"I'm going to make you pay for this, Violet."

"God, I hope so."

Once we start the workout, her smart mouth stops with the quips and hollers out encouragement instead. She usually runs me through the circuit, but today she joins me, and I find myself cheering for her just as much.

Exercise after exercise, rep after rep, we push each other.

Sweat pours down my back, pooling at the hem of my shirt and causing it to stick to me like a second skin. Zoe's skin is slick with moisture, glowing like a beacon. My fingers itch to pull her beneath me and crawl up her body, right here in the sand, to taste the sweet salt of her skin.

"Last one," she huffs, her breathing ragged as we approach the final circuit.

"We got this, babe."

"Yeah." Her eyes flash as she bends forward and braces her hands on her knees.

"You okay?" I ask.

She nods, her eyes trained on her sneakers. It's unlike Violet to be so winded. Then again, we did drink our body weight in rum last night. Maybe she's more hungover than I thought?

Then she straightens and tosses me her sassy smirk. "Let's do this, Hollywood."

Three minutes later, Violet and I are lying in the sand, our lungs sucking in ragged gulps of oxygen, our hearts exploding in our chests.

"You're a good trainer, Zoe," I murmur, my pinky finger brushing hers.

A pause hangs between us before Zoe hooks her pinky around mine. "I don't know how to do this with you, Eli." Her words are a confession, her tone more sincere than I've ever heard it.

At the sound of my name, I turn my face toward hers, tracing her profile in my mind. "Because there's an expiration date?"

"No, I'm fine with that."

I hate that her easy acceptance that we'll never work out irritates me. Obviously, we could never work out. For starters, there's the distance. Beyond that, I don't do serious relationships. Plus, she strikes me as the type of woman who does everything seriously. With intent. Purpose. With the best of intentions or not at all.

"Then what?"

"You're too… distracting."

Rolling my head back to look at the sky, I laugh. Really laugh, until I have to bring my knees up into my chest. Violet rolls toward me, and I turn my body so I'm facing her. I raise my hand to cup her cheek, grip the back of her neck, and bring her mouth to mine. Kissing her hard, I savor the heat that rolls off of her body, the cold sweat that drops from her pores into mine.

"I'm going to distract you in the best way possible, babe. Don't think too hard about how good things are between us. Easy and fun are a blessing, not a curse."

"Is that a promise?" she murmurs back, her eyes sparking with a seriousness I don't understand.

"Swear it."

DISTRACTING ZOE IS EASY.

Over the next two weeks, we fall into an understanding. At work, we're professional. During our training sessions, she pushes me to the brink, demanding every last ounce of my energy. But in my stretches of free time, I find myself drawn to her.

So much so that we start sharing meals, sneaking quickies in between shooting, spending our nights tangled in sheets, her leg pressed in between mine, her hair tickling my chest.

It's natural. Organic. The most effortless relationship I've casually fallen into in my life. Zoe's brightness could rival the sun's and her enthusiasm is infectious.

Instead of stressing over scenes, I find myself trying new approaches with abandon. Instead of worrying over the shit the media is printing, I don't even bother to read it.

With Violet, each moment is infused with its own brand of extraordinary, and I'm soaking it all up.

"What's your favorite movie?" I ask her one night.

She's seated at the table in my suite, working on her laptop after ending a FaceTime call with her dad.

"*Curious Case of Benjamin Button,*" she answers automatically.

"Seriously?" I scoff, stacking my feet on the coffee table and reclining on the couch. "Why?"

Turning to look at me, she shrugs. "It's strangely bittersweet. Like imagine if you could have all the wisdom of an adult and see the world through a child's eyes."

"But wouldn't that defeat the entire concept of seeing the world through a child's eyes?"

Zoe chews the corner of her mouth. "I see your point. But, I don't know, I loved that he had this great love. In a way, it was like two ships passing in the night. They both knew their lives would outpace their love. It forced them to be present in the moments, to appreciate the mundane."

"You do that."

"Do what?"

"Live in the moment. Close your eyes when you breathe in the salt of the sea. Take an extra moment to smell a flower or point out the shade of some random bird. You stare at your food like you're memorizing it before you take a first bite, and you wear a different pair of earrings every morning."

Zoe chuckles, turning back to her work. "I didn't realize you noticed all that."

"But then you know that you do it."

"Yeah."

"Why?"

"Why what?"

"When did you start noticing all the little things? You

can't say you've always been like this. Eventually everyone gets caught up in their own lives. The only people who are in tune to the little things are the ones who've had experiences that jogged their awareness."

Zoe's skin pales, her eyes dragging from mine to her computer screen. When she turns toward me again, a sassy smirk glances off her lips. "Then how do you explain yourself?"

"Me?"

"You noticed I change my earrings."

Smirking, I tap my hand against my chest. "Fair. Okay, so I'm learning through you. You've breathed this weird lightness into my life."

"*Really?*" Zoe drags out the word, her smile sly. She waves around the luxury suite we're sitting in. "This has nothing to do with it?"

"Come here." I beckon for her to join me on the couch.

She points to her computer. "Working."

"Come on, you have the rest of your life to work."

A shadow passes over her features and she dips her head, tucking her hair behind her ear. After a moment, she stands and saunters over to me .

"To answer your question, no. The suite, our surroundings, have nothing to do with it." I hook the top of my foot behind Zoe's thigh to inch her closer to me. "Maybe at first. When I first made it and had the funds to throw down on bottle service at the hottest clubs or the best tables in the trendiest restaurants, yeah. It was easy to feel like I was on top of the mountain. Especially since it was my hard work that made it possible, my money. When I found out about the inheritance from my dad, I didn't give a shit. I never touched any of it. But this, now, it's all you, babe." I jerk my foot forward so Violet stumbles and I can tug her over me. Lying on top of me, our chests rising and falling in sync, I palm the side of her face and study her.

The darker flecks of chestnut in her honey eyes, the tiny spray of freckles on the bridge of her nose, the slope of her cheekbones and the rosy color that tinges the apples of her cheeks at my touch.

Her eyes stray from mine to my mouth and back again and my chest tightens at the awareness of just how much she wants me to kiss her.

Our mouths hover inches apart, her lips plush and pink.

Her gaze darkens with each passing second. Heat sweeps through my stomach.

Wrapping my feet over her ankles, I anchor her to me, even though she hasn't made any attempt to wriggle out of my embrace.

"You're changing the game for me, Violet." I murmur the words, my chest tightening. My spine prickles with need for this woman, but before I go dropping truths, I need to know where her head's at. "Easy and fun is turning out to be more of a curse than I thought."

Slowly, her fingers trail up my chest, my neck, until the blunt edges of her nails scrape along my jaw. "I like this, Eli."

"What?" I lean into her touch.

"Everything you are." She inches closer, her eyes bleeding with a message I can't decipher.

Then she drops her lips to mine and I forget all about needing her words. The feel of her mouth moving over mine erases all logic.

My body hums with appreciation for hers. Her smoothness over my roughness, her softness over my hard planes. Her sweetness that dulls some of my harsh edges. Our kiss turns hungrier, needier. My hands track her face until I tangle them in her long hair, the scent of coconut wafting around us and centering me in this moment.

I kiss her with all the things I can't say because I don't want to go down this road again.

She takes my kiss, swallows my ugly vulnerabilities, and owns them like they're hers.

Flipping her beneath me, I straddle her and work her shirt over her head. Her full breasts fall free as I swipe her bra off in the same movement.

"You're irresistible." I drop my head to suck one raspberry nipple in my mouth.

She arches automatically, her hands digging into my scalp, keeping me anchored to her chest. "Make me feel it all, Eli. I want everything."

I flick my tongue over the pointy nub before moving to her other breast, lavishing it with the same attention.

"Break me apart," she whispers.

Moving lower, I taste the sweetness of her skin, my hands already working her leggings down her thighs. When my mouth collides with her panties, I growl, snapping them at her hip so they fall away and reveal her center like a long-awaited present.

"Let me drown in it."

I swipe my tongue down her core, slow and languid.

Zoe bucks once and I grip her thighs. "Make me forget."

Forget? Her words prickle at the back of my neck but I let them roll off my shoulders and focus on the moment instead. Burying my face between her legs, I devour her, enjoying every moan that falls from her lips. Each buck of her body drives me deeper, wild with need for everything she's giving to me.

She comes hard, like the roar of a crashing wave, cresting and breaking. Pulling back slightly, I slide two fingers deep inside her and watch the glow radiate from her skin as she rides her high. Her eyes are glassy when they connect with mine, her fingers trembling when they reach for me.

"Please, Eli. I need you." Her voice is broken, and it pulls at a thread in my chest, but I'm coiled too tightly, too needy for my own release.

"I got you, Violet. I've always got you." I press up onto my knees and position myself at her entrance. Holding her gaze, I push into her, relieved that we already had the conversation about birth control pills and clear STD screenings, and watch as her eyes flutter closed. Gathering her into my chest, I rock deeper.

"Fuck, baby. You feel so good." My palms push her hair away from her eyes as her nails dig into my shoulders.

Our combined breathing elevates into panting as I breathe secrets into her skin and she binds me to her with ribbons laced with deceit.

19
ZOE

Dancing in my underwear was something I used to do to cheer myself up. Especially on the hard days. The ones that marked memories of Mom. Her birthday. The date she died. A commercial for the newest installment in the *Toy Story* series, when the second film was the first one we saw together in theaters. If I close my eyes, I can still smell the popcorn and feel her presence beside me.

Little things, moments and memories and reminders, make ordinary days hard.

And if it's not my mom, it's my grandma. Or Dad's blindness. Or a slew of people unfollowing That Fit Bitch Life.

On those hard days where I feel desperation clawing up my throat, threatening to break free with a limitless supply of sobs, I crank up some party music as loud as the speakers allow and dance in my underwear.

Now, though, I'm dancing for an entirely different reason.

Hope fills the cracks in my chest. Excitement races through my veins like tiny messengers, desperate to have every cell on board, to make sure my entire being knows just how wonderful life feels right now. Even when doubt rears her annoying, albeit logical, head, the elation of my heart stomps her back down into the recesses of my mind.

Jamming out to Lizzo's *Good as Hell*, I shake my ass and allow myself to be fully present in this moment. Partly, I know it's because I'm soaking up experiences the way I collected stickers as a kindergartner — with an insatiable hunger. The other part is because Eli Holt makes me feel alive. Like my nerve endings are engaged with the freaking air I walk through.

The restlessness that usually rattles around my chest is gone. The worries and concerns I hold clenched in my fists have disappeared. All I hear is Lizzo, all I see is endless stretches of greenery and flowers, and all I feel is happy. Deliriously so.

In fact, it takes me a moment to realize that my phone is ringing, jarring the beat of the song. Glancing at Charlie's face, I swipe right until her picture is live.

"Hey hey!" I cheer, giving her some of my best moves.

Charlie erupts in laughter, clutching a pillow to her chest until she falls sideways on her bed. "God, I miss your dumb face."

"What's going on?" I grin, lowering the music and slipping on an oversized T-shirt before I perch on my bed.

"Nothing as exciting as a mid-day dance sesh."

"Yeah, well, you know how I do. How're things at Shooters?"

Charlie's brow furrows for a moment before smoothing back out. "Okay."

"Just okay?"

"Things are good with your dad," she hurries to reassure me. "Just, stupid shit with some drunk customers who can't keep their traps shut."

The forlorn expression that crosses her face causes me to

sit up straighter. It's unlike Charlie to be so bummed, especially by some douchey drunks…unless something is really wrong. "Charlie?"

She blinks, pulling her hair away from her mouth. "I'm fine. Sorry. Anyway, I wanted to call because *Gossip* reported that —"

"No," I shake my head, holding up a hand. "We haven't had a chance to really talk about what's going on in your life. Is there any chance Evan is the douchey drunk?"

Her face reddens and she chomps angrily on her ponytail, the way she does when she's stressed or feeling too many things at once.

"What's going on with you guys?" I ask softly.

"It's insane, isn't it?"

"What?"

"That we're sleeping with brothers."

I manage to smile at the fact that Eli and Evan are brothers. What are the odds? "I don't care who he is, he shouldn't be making you sad. What's going on? And when did you sleep with him?"

She sighs, "A week ago. Well, a week ago was the last time. It happened a few times the week before."

"And?"

"And…I thought we could date. Like normal people. Except after I spent the night at his house, he hustled me out the door at 4AM. I didn't even have my shoes on."

"What the hell? Why?"

"Something about his son."

"Ollie." I recall Eli's stories about his nephew, the cute little soccer player I met on FaceTime once.

"Ollie," Charlie confirms. "What is so awful about me that he wouldn't want his son to meet me?"

"Nothing. Charlie, it may not even be about you. Maybe

he's just not ready to introduce Ollie to a woman in his life," I point out.

"No, he said, 'You need to leave. Now. I can't have Ollie meeting you like this.'"

"Okay," I draw the word out, realizing that I would question those words if they fell from Eli's mouth too. "Maybe he meant he didn't want Ollie to meet you for the first time after you spent the night. Maybe it would be better if you came over during the day or —"

"That's what I thought too," she interrupts me, her eyes wide. "That makes sense. What doesn't make sense is that he cancelled our next date and completely blew me off the entire weekend… that is, until Sunday Night Football rolls around and I'm working, dealing with some drunk guys, you know, the usual stuff."

I nod.

"It got a little wild, but nothing I couldn't handle. And then he waltzes in, practically gets in a fight with a group of guys, and then scolds me in front of them. In front of the entire pub. Telling me that I should do better at putting them in their places. That the way I'm dressed is giving them other ideas." She throws up her hands, exasperated and hurt.

I gasp, my fingers lifting to my lips as I process her words.

There's no way Charlie would take kindly to someone insinuating she can't handle her own at Shooters. Especially not from a guy who blew her off and then implied she was flirting with customers. Sometimes, friendliness and a little banter is the easiest way to calm down a rowdy table.

"Damn, Charlie. That sucks. And not that I know Evan, but it doesn't sound like him at all. Eli's always talking about how professional and kind of uptight he is, what with dealing with the stress of his job and being a single parent."

"He was drunk," she admits, and I can tell that his drunkenness bothered her even more. "Now, he's blowing up my phone, all apologetic and 'let's have dinner.' And I'm just over it."

I tilt my head, studying her. "Are you sure?" I ask softly, knowing my best friend is way too affected to just be over it.

She scrubs her eyes with the heels of her hands. "I'm over never being good enough for the guys I date. Like, you don't want me to meet your son. You don't think I should work at a pub. You don't think I should wear such tight jeans. What the hell?"

"Did he say all that?" I ask, my attempt at trying to play devil's advocate and remain neutral dissolving in a cloud of anger.

"He didn't have to. It was implied," she bites out.

"Charlie, I don't know what to say. You deserve better than that. You deserve someone who's going to support your decisions, not tear them down."

She shakes her head, her voice angry. "No offense, but it's not like I want to bartend for the rest of my life."

"I know."

"But excuse me for not having a freaking law degree either."

"I know." I nod, because I do know. It's not easy attending community college part-time and staying in our hometown. There aren't any fancy jobs or even decent ones that earn good money, and the ones that exist in downtown Chicago require a hell of a lot more qualifications than Charlie currently has. Not that she's not working toward her degree, it's just life threw her a series of curveballs, and she's still recovering from them. "You okay?"

She nods, sniffling. "Yeah. I just, I thought he was different."

"Me too. Maybe he is." I whisper.

"I don't think so."

"Charlie, you're going to meet the right guy. These things happen when you least expect them."

"Yeah. I'm probably trying too hard, thinking every single date I have is going to be with *the one*."

"I love that you're a romantic."

"A hopeless one."

"Not hopeless." I smile. "Just optimistic."

She rolls her eyes. "Enough about Evan. And please don't tell Eli."

"Never!" I swear, somewhat offended by her assumption.

"Anyway, the reason I was calling is because *Gossip* reported a non-fabricated story. Gray Preston's ex-wife is Eli Holt's first love. His high school sweetheart. Natalie Beck."

"What?" I ask, taken aback.

Famous director Gray Preston married Eli's ex?

Natalie Beck. Her name tugs on my memory. "Are you sure?" I ask.

"Yes, do you remember her?"

"No." I shake my head, but something flickers at the edges of my memory. "Do you?"

"She was a senior when we were freshman. Eli graduated the year before her. She was a candy striper at —"

"The hospital. It was right before Mom died."

Charlie nods, her eyes watching me closely, waiting for my reaction.

I think back to that time, trying to see past the fog of grief that clouds all my memories of Mom's final year. "She was sweet. Always brought Mom extra Jell-O."

"The cherry ones."

"Mom liked her." I recall the tall blond with the striking blue eyes and natural elegance. She walked the hospital halls like she didn't really belong there, too exquisite to be surrounded by so much sorrow.

"Your mom liked everyone."

"Yeah." Mom really did like everyone. She was too good for the rest of us.

"I just thought it was weird. Like, too much of a coincidence."

"Yeah," I agree, "that is strange." I turn over this interesting turn of events. Eli dated Natalie, a girl from our hometown, a girl from our high school. For years. "Why'd they break up?"

"The article doesn't say."

"When?" I ask, my mind on overdrive, my skin suddenly heating as my stomach drops, although I don't understand why. He didn't do anything wrong. Obviously, he dated before me. But his high school sweetheart, the phrase keeps blinking in my mind. It seems like more than just dating; it seems deeper.

"Right before he moved out to L.A."

"Do you think that's why they broke up? Because he was leaving?"

"I don't know. All I know is that she recently divorced Gray, and *Gossip* is beefing up the story to pit Gray and Eli against each other on set."

"Because of Natalie? Eli's never even mentioned her. To my knowledge, he and Gray are super professional on set."

Charlie shrugs. The fact that she doesn't chime in with some witticism about Natalie not mattering irks me.

You're being ridiculous. Paranoid.

"Do you think he still cares about her?" I blurt out, not even caring that I've outed myself.

"Shit, Zo. You really care about him, don't you?"

Blowing out a miserable breath, I nod. "I knew dancing in my underwear for a happy reason was too good to be true."

"Hold up. You don't even know anything."

"I know Eli Holt was in love with Natalie Beck."

"Well, yeah, but maybe it was like puppy love."

I narrow my eyes and Charlie swears. "Just ask him about her," she suggests.

"That's the worst advice you've ever given me."

"No, the worst advice I ever gave you was to get a Brazilian the morning you decided to lose your virginity."

"Fuck, that hurt like a bitch." I wince, remembering the burning pain of my skin on top of the awkwardness of first-time sex. "You suck, Charlie."

"You love me, Zo."

"You really think I should ask him?"

"I do. Especially if you guys are going to move forward in your whatever-you're-calling-it relationship. You both should be able to talk openly about your pasts."

"Fine. But then you need to talk to Evan too. You're clearly upset about the way things went down between you guys, and if he's still popping into Shooters, that means he's coming to see you. So talk to him."

Charlie flips me the middle finger, but a moment later nods in acquiescence.

Flopping back onto my bed, I hold my iPhone over my head and stare at my best friend. "What if he's still in love with her?" I switch the subject back to Eli.

"Then it's a good thing you're asking him," she jokes, but I hear the undercurrent of concern in her tone.

And it worries me too.

Something pricks at the back of my neck as I walk down to the beach to meet Eli for his workout.

Nerves. A slick inadequacy that slips through my consciousness like slime, infecting everything it touches. Awareness that I'm lacking in so many ways compared to Brooke. And now Natalie.

Because, of course, I Googled her after hanging up with Charlie. Tall, graceful, and elegant, Natalie Beck filled my screen just the way I remembered her. Blonde hair, bright blue eyes, and breathtaking.

Guess Eli doesn't have a type; the three of us couldn't look any more different.

But still I feel less than.

Because they're established, financially flourishing, society revered women, and I'm the girl who would step into the ring with an MMA contender and think I stood a chance.

As my feet meet the sand, I spot Eli. He's stretching, his shoulder blades rippling under the thin material of his tank, the tendons in his arms pulsing as he hugs a forearm to his chest.

Jesus, he literally rivals the ocean view, so much so that I don't even notice the spray of seashells and greenery that once held my attention captive. Instead, I'm captivated by Eli, absolutely beguiled by him.

Breathing in the ocean wind, I let it unfurl through my body, slowing my galloping heart. I can ask Eli about his ex-girlfriend, can't I? I mean, he's fucked me in public, kissed me sweetly in his shower, and asked me my favorite movie. Doesn't that mean I can ask him this?

My fingernails dig into the flesh of my palms. I hate that I didn't know he had a high school sweetheart. Someone from my high school. Someone my mom liked. Someone he dated when he was sixteen years old until right before his career took off.

My longest relationship lasted a whole five months, and we were more study buddies who liked to hook up than a love match.

With Brooke, it's easier to understand their history. He mentions her casually, doesn't seem rattled by working with her, and she's only been friendly and sweet to me when our paths have crossed on set or in the hotel.

She's out in the open, someone I see him interact with and watch as they both instantly turn off any passionate glances or gentle caresses the second "cut" is called on set.

But Natalie. He never mentioned her. Not even once. Why would he? Because she's Gray's ex-wife? Because she doesn't mean anything to him anymore? Or because he still harbors feelings for her and doesn't want anyone to know?

As much as I try to hold myself to some higher standard that wouldn't frantically click through *Gossip's* website like a rat in a New York dumpster, my curiosity won out.

I clicked. And clicked. Devoured article after article.

I saw the photos of a young, lanky Eli with his arm wrapped around Natalie, her blue eyes wide with wonder. The ones where she's straddling him in a booth in Shooters that someone must have swiped off Facebook. And then, the devastating, truly lost expression haunting Eli when he sees Natalie in the arms of Gray at a L.A. restaurant three years ago.

The ugly twist of his lips, the harshness of his jawline, the tightness in his shoulders, all spoke of a man scorned. But his eyes, oh God, his beautiful eyes bled pain. Betrayal. Ruin.

Natalie Beck broke Eli Holt. Maybe even shattered him. And now, the pieces that fill my vision, comprising the sexiest man I've ever seen, may not be whole enough to confess that he's still in love with her.

"Jesus, Violet. I don't have all day," he calls out, tapping the front of his Apple Watch.

Forcing a smile, I jog over to him. "I'm ready."

"Better be. I got a lot of stress to release." He grasps the top of his shoe behind his back to stretch out his quad.

"Stress? What stress?" My voice quivers and Eli's brow dips.

He lifts his chin in my direction. "Haven't been inside you in over twenty-four hours, babe. That shit's dangerous."

Snorting, I push his bicep, my fingers curling around his muscle in admiration, my nerves spiking for a completely different reason.

"Tonight, then?"

"Hell yeah."

"Okay." I worry my bottom lip back and forth between my teeth, my hand still holding his arm.

"What's going on, babe? You're thinking too hard," Eli says easily, unaware that my mind is literally imploding with thoughts of his past.

Jesus, Zoe. Grow up.

"Can we talk first?"

Eli stops moving and peers down at me, a flash of concern in his green eyes. "Sounds serious."

I squint up at him as the sun illuminates his presence, large and looming, big enough to swallow me whole, intense enough to burn me to ash.

"What's going on, Zo?" He steps closer and I drop my hand from his arm.

"Not now. Tonight. Later. I just…we have work to do now." I walk toward the equipment, but Eli's hand shoots out and circles my wrist, forcing me to look at him.

"Are you okay?" he asks seriously, his mouth pressing into a thin line.

"Really, it's nothing. I just, I want to get to know you better."

He studies me for a long beat. I can hear the wheels in his mind turning, considering, assessing. "What'd you read?" He asks, and my mouth drops open before a stream of laughter escapes.

"How'd you do that?"

"I've been in this game for a minute." He drops my wrist and tugs on the back of his neck. The sun glances off his tanned skin, sweat dotting his shoulders, his strength glistening like an aura. "What do you want to know?" His tone is curt, and I don't like the accusation in his words. As if I've already made my mind up about a million things and aren't approaching him for his truth.

Sighing, I shake my arms out at my sides. "I know Natalie."

Eli rears back as if I slapped him. "Know her?"

I chew the corner of my mouth, the memories of that time in my life, the ones where my mother was bald and frail and so damn resilient, flicker through my mind like a movie reel. "She was a candy striper at the hospital where my mom, when she…" I trail off, glancing back up.

Eli's expression transforms. The stoic, silent irritation from a moment ago cracks into understanding mixed with compassion. "I'm sorry, Zoe. I had no idea; I didn't even think…" He shakes his head. "I forgot she did that. It was only for a few months, and then she decided she didn't want to become a nurse after all."

I offer a tight smile, a torrent of unexpected tears squeezing my throat, burning behind my nose. It's still difficult for me to recall any memories from that period of my life and not cry.

I held onto my hope desperately, with everything I had until the very end. When Mom passed, all the hope I ever had disappeared like a big black hole, sucking away all the dreams and happiness I once took for granted and replacing it with darkness. A midnight so severe it took several years for me to paint a dawn.

"Violet." Eli's voice is low, almost husky.

I blink, and he comes back into focus as the long hospital hallways and the stench of antibacterial gel fade from my mind.

"We should work out." I clear my throat.

Eli nods, his eyes wary as they pass over my face. Reaching into his pocket, he pulls out his wallet and passes me a key card to his suite. "I have a meeting after this, but tonight, tonight we'll talk. Okay?"

His strong gaze, coupled with his gentle tone, settles me once more. I exhale, feeling my footing return as I gesture toward the workout equipment set up a few paces away. "Okay."

20

ELI

My confusion from Violet's confession has snowballed into total bafflement by the time she appears in my penthouse with the key I slipped her at our workout session.

Her hair is still wet, the ends drying into messy waves. Colorful yoga pants hug her hips and a long-sleeve tee hangs off one shoulder, tucked casually into the right side of her pants. She's wearing flip-flops, her toes a hot pink.

The right side of my mouth tugs up as I drink her in. My dick stirs to life, my mind fills with a barrage of questions, my entire being gravitates toward this beautiful woman who is so unlike anyone I've ever met.

"You look beautiful, Zoe." I walk toward her, my sweats hanging low on my hips, my chest bare. Stepping into her space, one hand automatically settles on her back as I lean down and brush a kiss across her cheek.

She inhales audibly, her back straightening. I fight a grin. I love that I still affect her this way, even after countless nights fucking her in every position known to humankind and stretches of daybreak hugging her against my chest, a simple kiss on her cheek still causes her breath to catch, her eyes to widen.

"I look like a hungover college kid. Harlow talked me into drinks." Her tone is casual even though I know my compliment pleases her.

"Come on in. I ordered room service." I walk into the living room, Zoe trailing me.

"Holy shit, Holt. What'd you order? The entire menu?"

Shrugging, I gesture for her to take a seat.

We both sit on the floor, the coffee table littered with four different entrees and a few appetizers between us. "Honestly, I'm starving." I admit, digging into a vegetable spring roll.

"Same." Zoe replies, her mouth already stuffed with crab meat. "How was your meeting?"

"Pretty good. It was just with Gray to discuss the film, some of the artistic elements he's thinking of using."

"He wanted your opinion?"

Snorting, I point my fork at her. "I'm more than just a pretty face and a sexy body, you know."

She throws a balled-up napkin at me, missing completely. "Coulda fooled me." She wiggles her eyebrows, holding up a long noodle with her fingers and dropping it into her mouth.

"Classy." I reach over to steal some noodles off her plate.

She pushes her plate closer and the gesture, so subtle, warms me from the inside out. This, this right here, the casual, easygoing, natural exchange of conversation over no-fuss food, eaten on the floor off a coffee table is why I'm so drawn to Zoe Clark. She's everything I never knew I wanted, and nothing like I've ever had.

We eat in easy silence for a few moments before Zoe clears her throat. Glancing up, she offers me a sheepish, almost apologetic smile. "You want to know about Natalie?" I offer.

Zoe nods. I don't miss how her knuckles turn white from her death grip on her fork.

I take a quick swig of my sparkling water. "Why're you so nervous, babe?"

"I don't know. It's just, you never mentioned her and I read —"

My eyebrow quirks up. I didn't know Zoe followed all the stupid gossip sites.

"Charlie sent me an article," she huffs, flicking her wrist by way of explanation. "If it was anyone else, I would have dismissed it, but Natalie…" The way she says Natalie's name, her voice aching with a sadness I don't understand, causes the quip on the tip of my tongue to dissolve.

"So this is more about Natalie than me?" I ask uncertainly, watching Zoe closely.

"She…she was nice to my mom," she says, her eyes filling with tears.

Her voice, her beautiful face brimming with a hurt so overwhelming, steals my breath, causes my entire body to ache. "Oh baby." I reach out a hand, cupping her cheek. "I'm so damn sorry."

"I…I like you, Eli. More than I ever thought I would." She clears her throat, and I remember how she straight up told me she wasn't looking for someone to stick around that first night I kissed her.

"I set the bar pretty low," I joke.

"True." She wipes her mouth with a napkin, a tiny chortle escaping, but then she blinks and her eyes grow serious. "I know you've had some really public relationships. You've never fed them with fodder, but you've never kept them secret either."

"Like with Brooke."

"Exactly. But with Natalie, I mean, I had no idea you

even dated her. And then, I learn that you guys were together for years. And that she married and divorced Gray, the director of this film. And I know her. Kind of." She stresses the last part and an image of Natalie, dressed in her candy striper uniform, her face open and carefree, flickers in my mind.

She loved volunteering. She did it for months.

Eventually, losing her patients wore on her. She grew sadder, more anxious, unable to separate her role as a volunteer from her feelings as a person watching others suffer. So she quit.

Hearing Zoe speak about her, hearing her share how much her mom liked Natalie, allows me to remember Natalie the way she was. Before.

Before the fights and the jealousy. Before the pregnancy and the abortion. Before all the toxicity burned whatever good was between us. And before only the guilt of the past was the binding that held us together. Continues to connect us today.

"Why would you work for the ex-husband of your ex-girlfriend, your high school sweetheart?"

"He's one of the best directors of his time," I explain, my respect for his work no secret. "Besides, how would it look if I turned down the role, the opportunity to expand my brand and learn from one of the best, because of a girl I dated in high school?"

"So you did want to turn it down? You were just scared about what people would think?"

I sigh, pinching the bridge of my nose.

"There's more to this story," she says, an unmistakable confidence in her tone. Her eyes nearly plead with me to be honest, and my stomach sinks at her intuition.

"It was a business decision, babe. The movie truly was a

business decision. But everything else —" I pause, collecting my thoughts.

"Eli, please." Her voice breaks. When I glance into her face, I see shadows I don't understand.

Swearing softly, I incline my head toward hers. "Look, Natalie and me, we're complicated. There's a lot of history there, and a lot of hurts and —"

"Do you still love her?"

"What?" My head snaps back up and I breathe in Zoe's tortured expression.

"Do you still love her?" She repeats the question, her voice strong even as her eyes swirl with hurt.

This is it. The moment where I need to eat all my fucking lies from earlier or own them and forge ahead.

Zoe squares her shoulders, staring at me with a hardness that causes my chest to ache even though I'm impressed at how calmly she handles herself. She's a goddamn warrior, never flinching from my gaze.

"I'm not in love with her," I finally admit, the confession coloring the air between us. "I haven't been in love with her for a long, long time."

"So then why did you keep her a secret? Why didn't you tell me about her? Is it because we're just casual?" Hurt wraps around her tone as vulnerability flares in her eyes.

"No."

"Is it because of Gray?"

"Gray?"

"Out of respect for him? His marriage?"

"No." I shake my head. "I didn't tell you about her because she doesn't matter anymore. A long time ago, I did love her. I thought she was the goddamn sun, and I orbited around her like the forgotten planet of Pluto."

"Pluto's not a planet anymore."

"Exactly."

"I don't understand —"

"She had an abortion." The words rip from my throat, coming out jangled and incoherent.

"*What?*"

"We were having a baby." I work a swallow, hating that the truth still cuts, that just admitting the words out loud picks at so many wounds with too many layers of scabs. "And she terminated it."

The shock that blooms in Zoe's expression is almost like sweet relief. It flickers across her face in varying degrees before her eyes take on a haunted glow. Her fingers curl into her hands, nails scratching against the top of the coffee table. "And you wanted the baby?"

"A whole basketball team of them." My voice is raspy, longing for a truth I'm reluctant to admit. I may have let it slip during our game of Two Truths and a Lie, but now I'm confiding in her for real. Sharing a truth I haven't been able to tell anyone, not even Evan. "I want a family. I've always wanted a family, to be a real dad. The opposite of the non-example I had growing up until Mom married Derek."

My hand curls around my sparkling water, just for something to hold, as I admit the rest. "Natalie broke us, broke a part of me, when she had an abortion. Not because I wouldn't have supported her decision. I would have. I know it was hers to make. But because she didn't even tell me she was planning to do it, I never got to process anything while it was happening, only after. And that hurt."

My hand moves to my chest, the heel of it digging in, deeper and deeper, searching for something solid to settle on. "I thought we were more than that. A handful of months later,

I left Chicago and my career took off. After that, she moved to L.A., and she met Gray." I spit his name, staring right at Zoe. "Gray Preston is the best in the business. He was the best four years ago too. He swept her off her feet, and she never looked back. Except on the nights when she couldn't handle her own guilt. The nights when she was a new bride, and instead of warming her husband's bed, she hit the bottle and called me, sobbing. I never hung up the phone first or ignored one of her calls until the night I met you." I admit, hating myself for how long I enabled Natalie's behavior without ever providing the help she really needed. Hating myself for still not confiding in Gray that his ex-wife, his then-wife, needed more support than he could ever understand. Hating myself for not always taking her calls and sometimes leaving her hanging since I became captivated by Zoe Clark.

"Why?" she whispers, her tongue darting out to wet her lips. "Why would she still call you when she married Gray?"

"Because I was the only person who could understand the depth of the pain she felt, of the guilt she carried."

"But didn't she hurt you?"

"We hurt each other. A lot. Our relationship was tumultuous and toxic. We tore each other down and then built each other back up just to tear down again. But she's the mother of my unborn child. The least I can do for her is not turn my back when she needs someone to listen." My hand clenches, the sparkling water sloshing over the rim and spilling onto the table. "And I'll stand by that."

"I'm sorry." Zoe's eyes track the drops of water, the tiny trail of bubbles on my hand.

"For what?"

"Your loss." She looks up, her honey eyes so damn empathetic that I burn with emotions I don't know how to express.

"Thank you. One day, I'm going to make a lot of babies with a woman who is as eager and desperate to be a mama as I am to be a dad. And then, I'm going to be the best goddamn daddy there is."

"I believe you."

21

ZOE

Eli's confession rocks my world, throwing me off-balance, changing the center of gravity.

The floor shifts beneath me, the air pulses with an energy I've never felt, and time slows. The drops of water on his wrist glisten, the noodles on my plate transform into a complicated puzzle, and the sound of my pulse in my ears blocks out everything else. My fingers tremble and I tuck them in my lap, wringing my hands together.

Eli wants babies. A whole basketball team.

He wants babies.

It's different now, hearing him say the words, seeing the devastating expression on his face, than it was the night at the bar. This isn't a game; this is his heart's desire.

The backs of my eyes burn and my throat seems incapable of forming words, just a strangled groan I swallow back.

Fuck.

My heart shatters, fragmented chunks of longing exploding into pieces of resentment that disintegrate into heartbreak.

I will never bear children. Not even for a man as powerful as Eli Holt. Not even for a heart as desperate as my own.

"Hey." His voice sounds far-off, as if he's speaking to me underwater. I look up, my eyes searching for his gaze until I'm drowning in two pools of green, wondering if I even want to find oxygen. "You okay, baby? I know that was a lot. I-I'm sorry."

"For what?" I whisper, scraping my palms along the underside of the table, trying to anchor myself to something tangible. Does he know? Does he suspect?

"I unloaded on you and, well, it's a lot."

"I'm fine."

"You don't look fine."

"Is it cold in here?" I blurt out, my eyes scanning the room for an open window or an ice storm or something that would make sense of the fact that shivers are wracking down my spine.

"Violet." Eli must move because in the next blink, he's crouching next to me, his hand massaging the small of my back, his eyes boring into mine with so much concern I could cry.

His eyes are hypnotizing, laying bare a thousand truths, secrets to a life I'll never share. But for this one moment, staring into the depth of emotions swirling in his green eyes, I let myself freefall.

My hands stop their desperate tapping against the table and cup his cheeks instead. The stubble that grazes my palms roots me to the moment. My eyes flutter closed and I feel Eli's exhale fan across my lips, like a soft breeze. I lean into him, and the air between us shrinks as he moves closer, his mouth arcing over mine like a shooting star.

I make a wish. *The wish.*

His lips touch mine, instantly pulling me under.

The kiss is slow, languid, and careful in a way we've never been with each other. He tastes my mouth with purpose, taking time to enjoy the dance of my tongue with his. Slowly, he shifts until he can lie me down, cradling my frame in between his arms, shielded from everything as he hovers over me. Tucked between the coffee table and the couch, all I can see is Eli, the solemnity of his expression, the reassurance in his gaze.

Reaching back, he tugs the T-shirt he threw on before dinner over his head and discards it. Hard muscle and tanned skin ripple. My fingers trace his abs appreciatively as he yanks my shirt lower on my shoulder and dips his head, pressing kisses mixed with nips up the side of my neck. I turn my head to the side, giving him more access, breathing in his scent and letting his warmth fill me up.

His hands touch me with a reverence I've never known, quieting my doubts and pulling me further into his orbit. My thighs fall to the sides as he settles between them, the weight of his body sheltering me with a security I've yearned for.

Eli pulls back slightly, his eyes focused on one of mine before switching to the other, as if gauging my reaction, confirming that so much more is happening, unfolding, joining under the surface of our physical connection.

"You can always ask me for the truth, Violet." His words are raspy, gravel and sand and a million tiny things that create the big things. The ones worth living for. "I won't lie to you."

My heart pangs in my chest. A reminder. A warning.

I haven't been honest with him. I've shared the darkest of lies, hoping that I could believe in them.

No, I haven't been honest with anyone. Not even myself.

My lips part, and the confession beads on the tip of my tongue, ready to explode forth in the quietest of whispers, but

Eli's mouth captures mine once more. I allow him to swallow my truth along with my fear.

Relief erupts, washing through my limbs like a salve. My hands move to the back of his neck, my fingertips grazing his hair. His mouth is hot against my skin, his touch certain. He undresses me slowly, as if we have all the time in the world. Moments and decades to explore each other's bodies, to fall into each other's minds, to join our souls and blossom into something greater than our individual selves.

His gaze drags over my skin, inch by inch. His eyes darken, his lids grow heavier, and I feel the appreciation like a caress. "You're so goddamn beautiful."

"Kiss me, Eli. And don't ever stop." I guide his face back to mine before my hands drop to the waistband of his sweats.

In mere moments, we're naked, our bodies pressed together, melding into one another with a thousand promises I'll break by week's end. In this moment, though, even that doesn't matter. All that matters is him. And me. And us.

Eli grips my hip, his mouth trailing down my chest, along my stomach, peppering kisses the entire time until he finds my core, wet and desperate for his touch.

A growl falls from his mouth in the same moment a sigh drops from mine. Anticipation squeezes my stomach, my body nearly trembling as I connect with his gaze. Filled with more than just lust, the depth of his emotion undoes me. Keeping his eyes on mine, his tongue darts out, licking a path right up my center.

"Eli," I whisper, entranced by him.

He doesn't respond, just grips my thighs harder, parting them, and buries his face between my legs in the most delicious torture I've ever experienced.

"Fuck." I drop my head back, my fingers tangled in his hair. "Eli."

His tongue parts me slowly, seductively, longingly. My body tightens and trembles as he moves even slower. Desperate for more, my mouth parts and then, I feel his fingers enter me. One, two, three.

Fuck.

His mouth travels to my clit, licking and nipping and sucking while his fingers pump in and out in a steady rhythm.

My eyes close, my hips bucking off the floor, but Eli's weight keeps me steady as my senses heighten. Colors explode in my mind like fireworks, my core tightening, my body shaking.

"Baby, I'm —" I can't even get the words out, consumed with sensations that are stronger, deeper, bigger than anything I've ever felt before. "Eli —"

"Come for me, baby."

His strangled command pushes me over the edge. Waterfalls burst through me, a flood of pleasure that seems endless in its intensity. I cry out as Eli drags one last lick through my center.

"Oh God," I murmur, returning to reality.

Glancing down, he's perched casually between my thighs, grinning at me like a goddamn quarterback who threw the winning touchdown.

"Like your sounds, babe," he smirks.

"Jesus." I drop my head back once more.

In the next moment, Eli distracts me again. Slides into me like it's the most natural thing in the world, like we fit together perfectly, like we were made for each other. My heart stutters in my chest, overwhelming emotions rising in me like high tide. Gripping Eli closer, I press kisses over his shoulders and bury my face in the crook of his neck. Losing myself to his touch, the sensations they elicit, I break apart in his arms once more.

"You okay, Violet?" he asks me afterwards.

After I gave him a blow job to rival all blow jobs in the steam of his shower, the water beating down on us, his fingers locked in my hair. After we had sex again, this time with my back pressed against the shower wall, the tiles chafing against my skin. After we were forced to shower all over again and I kissed him hard when I realized he bought the coconut shampoo I like. After we toweled off and I rang out the ends of my sopping wet hair while he used his forearm to clear the steam from the mirror.

Standing in his ridiculous bathroom, a towel hangs low on his hips and the cutest grin glances off his lips. Lips that devoured me with an insatiable hunger. One that was more than just physical.

Deeper than just like. One that was different than anything I ever experienced.

"Truth?" I look up, meeting his eyes in the reflection of the bathroom mirror.

"Please." He turns and slides onto the vanity, his thigh next to my hand.

Reaching out, I place my palm on his thigh and grip the terrycloth of the towel. "I know this is supposed to be fun. Not complicated. A hook-up for our time in the Seychelles. But I like you, Eli Holt. And it scares the hell out of me."

His grin grows cockier, his chest puffing out slightly. But his eyes, they search mine out with a vulnerability I want to hold onto as he opens his mouth and murmurs, "I've been there for a while now, baby."

22

ELI

"It's different with her." I explain to my brother on FaceTime.

"Different how?" He narrows his eyes but he's grinning. I know he's happy for me even though he can't help but worry. I don't have a great track record with women.

"I just feel like we've spent time getting to know each other."

"It's barely been two months."

"On an island where we spend a ridiculous amount of time in each other's company."

"I guess," Evan says, but his tone holds a note of skepticism that bothers me. "Just…be careful, Eli."

"She's different, Evan. I'm telling you. Violet is nothing like Natalie."

"Yeah, well, Natalie wasn't always like Natalie either," my brother murmurs. "Or Sophie."

I wince, knowing how difficult it is to even say his ex-wife's name.

At this point, I think it bothers Evan more that she left Ollie than him. That even if Sophie didn't want him, she should have still chosen her son. Stuck around for Ollie if not for anyone else. And he's right.

I hate how parents manipulate their kids for their own gain. When I have kids, I'm going to show up for them, every single day. Put their needs ahead of my own. You know, *parent*.

"How's Ollie?" I ask, switching the topic to the world's best nephew.

Evan brightens immediately. "Man, he's awesome. Doing great in school. Scored two goals last week. Indoor soccer now."

"Damn, I wish I was there."

"Yeah, Connor surprised him at his last game and got some good photos. I'll ask him to send them your way. Oh, and thank you for the sea turtle pictures and stuffed animal you sent. Ollie sleeps with it every night."

I laugh, swiping a beer off the coffee table and relaxing back into the couch. "I'm glad he likes it." I take a swig. "Tell me about home. Are you dating anyone?"

Evan freezes, as if I asked him something I shouldn't have. I shift in my seat.

"Who is she?" I press.

He shakes his head and sighs. "No one worth mentioning now."

I raise an eyebrow.

"It burned out before it had an opportunity to properly take off," he says by way of explanation before launching into a story about one of his cases.

I open my mouth to dig deeper, but he speaks over me and I let the topic drop.

As Evan fills me in on his life, his work, and shares jokes from Ollie, I find myself hanging onto his every word. Grinning. Laughing. Enjoying his stories with a desire to hear more.

My mind wanders. What would it be like if Zoe and I moved back home? Together? Could we raise a baby there, near his or her cousin Ollie? Would they play soccer together?

I could help Zoe's dad out at Shooters. She could continue to work the MMA training circuit while I was on location, filming.

We could make this work.

A whole world of possibilities expands in my head, coloring my mind with the kind of future I always wanted and was too scared to hope for after Natalie.

But with Zoe, everything seems possible.

Everything is within reach, as long as I'm doing it with her by my side.

"Hey sexy." I snap my towel against her ass as she steps out of my rain shower. Leaning back against the counter, still sporting the hair and makeup look from set, I'm ready to rinse off and crawl in bed with my girl.

"Hey yourself." She forces a smile, a cough interrupting her words.

Frowning, I step closer, peering into her pale face. Her eyes are watery, the tip of her nose red. I brush some of her wet hair out of her face. "You okay?"

Zoe sighs, pinching the bridge of her nose. "I think it's just sinuses. I feel off."

"You're probably run-down. Burning that midnight oil."

She snorts, a foghorn in the empty bathroom. "Yeah, who's fault is that?"

I smirk, dropping a robe around her shoulders. "Go get in bed. I'm going to rinse off really fast, and then I'll bring you a tea and whatever magazine is lying around."

"Ooh, I hope it's *Gossip*." She grins over her shoulder, sashaying to the master bedroom.

"Take that back!" I call after her, grinning like a lunatic.

Zoe laughs, the sound of her lightness trailing back to the bathroom. Shaking my head at her retreating figure, I strip down and jump in the shower. The hot water rains down and I finally relax from a long day of shooting.

Playing Dr. Henry Shorn, absorbing his fears, portraying his uncertainties, is more mentally taxing then I anticipated. It makes me think about Violet's dad and how he managed to raise an incredible daughter while re-learning how to just exist in the world. That would all be devastating enough without grieving for his wife or opening a new business. When I think of the man I've met in passing at Shooters, never knowing he was Violet's dad, or who Zoe even was, I can't help but be impressed.

Deep in thought, I step out of the shower and wrap a towel around my waist. By the time I make it into the bedroom, ready to have another serious discussion with Zoe — one that delves more into the possibility of us being a couple after the movie wraps — her light snores pierce the air.

She's passed out, still clad in the hotel robe, her hair soaking wet. Grinning at her sweet face, I tug one of my T-shirts over her head and wrap her in an extra blanket, relieved that I'll be slipping into bed next to her tonight.

"Good morning, sunshine." Zoe greets me the next morning, her hair piled in a tangle on top of her head.

"I like your hair." I lean over the kitchen island, sipping my coffee.

Zoe flips me off and I snort.

"I was exhausted last night."

"I know, babe. How're you feeling today?"

Zoe pours herself a cup of coffee and rests her back against the kitchen counter. My T-shirt hits her mid-thigh, and even though she's a train wreck she still looks so adorable that I can't help but trail my gaze down her toned legs. "Eyes up here, Hollywood."

I look up, a blaze of concern spiking when I take in her paleness. "You okay?"

She gulps her coffee. "Yeah, I don't know. I feel strange, just…off somehow." She pushes her hair out of her eyes, grimacing as her knuckles snag on a tangle. "I feel exhausted."

"Not pregnant, are you?" I joke, although I don't hate the idea.

I don't hate it at all and that's the problem.

Zoe blanches, shaking her head. "Definitely not that." It's a whisper, threaded with unease.

"I'm kidding, Violet. Probably just a bug. Let's call off our workout today so I can nurse you back to health."

"Get out of here." She reaches into a tin to retrieve a muffin, takes a nibble, and tosses the rest to me. "You need to get to work. And so do I."

"Don't push yourself too hard."

"I'm not. I'm going to grab smoothies with Harlow in a bit."

"Have dinner with me tonight?"

"Duh."

Chuckling, I slip off the barstool and round the corner, my hands going to either side of Violet's hips, caging her in. I can count the freckles that spread across her nose, more vivid now against the paleness of her skin. "I have an idea."

"Oh yeah?" She looks up, her eyebrow quirking, a teasing smirk on her lips. "Enlighten me."

"I'm still working out the logistics."

"Maybe I can help." She chews the corner of her mouth, batting her eyelashes like a flirt.

God, why is being with her so much fun? Even the hard parts, like talking about our future. Even the parts I dreaded and avoided with every woman I've dated since Natalie, are exciting with Zoe.

"We've got, what, two more months here?"

She nods, her body stilling, her eyes growing serious.

"I don't want to give you up, my baby." I move one hand to her hip, inching the material of the T-shirt up until I can slip my hand underneath, feel her skin against mine.

"What do you mean?" Her voice is low, hesitant.

"I mean, I want to make this real between us. I want us to figure out how to make it work so we can both flourish in the jobs we love but still come home to each other at the end of the day. I want to be with you."

Her eyes widen, surprise blooming in her expression. "You're serious?"

"Very." I tug her hips against mine and when she feels my erection, she grins.

"You want to be my boyfriend?" she clarifies.

"I don't care what you call it, babe. As long as you're in my bed at the end of the day and we both know there's no one else. Just us."

"Just us," she repeats, a smile breaking across her face like sunshine after a long winter. "I like just us."

"I like you." I drop my mouth to hers, kissing her sweetly.

But the sweet quickly morphs into spice, and forty-minutes later, I walk onto set thirty minutes late without a care in the world. Because I left my girl completely sated on top of the kitchen counter.

And she's agreed to be mine.

23

ZOE

The hot water feels good against my skin after two intense workouts with Eli.

The first happened during our circuit training on the beach. The second, in my bed, just before Eli left for a dinner with his publicist.

My body, now sore and sated, totally relaxed, stills beneath the showerhead, breathing in the steam.

It's been nearly a week since Eli's confession. Since he whispered sweet words against my skin, spread me out on his kitchen countertop, and made me his.

For keeps.

Charlie nearly had an aneurysm, dancing around the bar like a showgirl, complete with jazz hands and twirls. Poor Fred thought she lost her mind.

Tonight, I'm FaceTiming with Dad to tell him all about my new beau. The one he's apparently known for years and has never mentioned. It would be so Dad to not give a shit that a Hollywood actor frequents his pub.

Laughing as I imagine his reaction to my news — "I'm

coming home next month with a boyfriend. You know, Eli Holt?" — I reach for my shower gel, completely forgetting that it's empty and I was supposed to buy more.

Tossing the empty bottle out of the shower, I swipe the bar of soap Eli uses instead.

And then, it happens.

It happens, and I freeze, the steam suddenly blinding, the water sharp, whipping my skin angrily.

"No." I spread the suds around my chest again.

I feel it. Again.

As small as a pea. As hard as a marble.

A bump.

A *lump*.

My body stills immediately, the soap dropping from my hand. I follow its fall, feel the spray of water as it shoots over my lower legs. Think about how dangerous it would be if I slipped.

I should pick up the soap, but my fingers are still feeling around my left breast.

Did I imagine it? No.

Is it what I think it is? Yes.

Fear that's been sleeping dormant in the epicenter of my stomach for over a decade wakes up and roars. My body burns hot and cold.

The water lashes at my skin, angry and painful. Flipping the faucet, I stand in the steam, my mind racing.

I feel again, the flesh of my breast ballooning around my finger as I dig the tip deep into my skin.

I hit the hard ball and swear, tears filling my eyes.

I knew this would happen. Haven't I known it for years?

The shrill ringing of my cell phone from the bathroom vanity causes me to jump. Stumbling from the shower, I wrap a towel around me and close my eyes, my tears coming harder, when I see Eli's name on the screen.

I knew this would happen. I've known it all along.

Ignoring his call, I hold my towel tighter and walk into my room. The cool air slaps me in the face as my thoughts rush forward, tripping over each other in their demand to be considered.

Call Dad.

No, don't do that. You'd break his heart.

You don't know anything yet. It could be benign.

Yeah, right. Hello naive, meet ignorant.

Tell Eli.

No, don't tell him anything. He won't understand.

Charlie?

What time is it in Chicago?

My phone beeps and I glance down at the screen.

Reminder: Call Dr. Salinas.

Closing my eyes, I exhale, tears burning in their desire to escape.

Sitting on the edge of my bed, I scroll through my contacts and press Send.

ME: Hey, I'm feeling like crap. I'm going to crash. Enjoy your dinner with Helen and I'll see you in the morning.

Eli: You okay? Let me take you to the doctor I suggested. You've been fighting this sinus infection for too many days.

Me: I'm fine. I just need a good night's sleep.

Eli: I'm finishing up now. I'll come to you.

Me: You're sweet. I would love nothing more than your naked Adonis body in my bed, but I don't want to get you sick. You've got a stacked week with shooting.

Eli: I don't care. I don't want you to be alone when you're not feeling right.

Me: I promise to message if I need anything. Swear it.

Two minutes tick by slowly, like I'm watching each grain of sand drop through an hourglass.

Eli: Okay, babe. I'm here if you need anything — ANYTHING. Now get that fine ass in bed and have sweet dreams.

Me: XOXO

Sighing, I scroll to Dad's contact info.

Me: Hey Daddy. Hope you're having a great day. I know we're supposed to catch up tonight, but I'm fighting a bug and can't keep my eyes open. We'll chat this week for sure. Miss you. XO

I hate texting my dad since I know it requires an extra step on his part to have the text processed and read aloud, but I also know if I talk to him tonight, I'll break down. I'm not ready to tell him yet.

I crawl into bed and stare at the ceiling, knowing sleep won't find me.

It doesn't.

Not for many hours as I lie in the darkness, my mind racing.

The stupid white paper with my BRCA results taunts me from across the room, tucked into my desk drawer. Except I know it's there, flashing like a neon sign that won't burn out.

I need to tell Dad. We've talked weekly since I came to the Seychelles, but our conversations have been more like check-ins instead of chats. Only now, I need to check in with the most important news of my life.

Slow your roll. It could be nothing.

Oh God. What if this is it? I've finally gone and done it. I've fallen for a Hollywood megastar, and now I have to let him go.

I have to tell Eli the truth.

Hell no, I'd mess up his entire film, his career. I know, just *know*, if he knew the truth, he'd want to help me. To be here for me.

Except he can't. He's in the middle of production on the film that's going to change his life.

Jesus. I need to talk to Charlie. Yes, tomorrow I'll call Charlie.

I finally doze off around 3AM, but when my alarm sounds at five sharp and my body shrieks in protest, my heartbeat thumping in my temples, my throat burning when I swallow, I roll over and send a message to Eli instead of standing from bed.

Me: Hollywood, I need to push our morning training until tonight. 6PM?

Eli: Baby, how sick are you? What's going on? I'm coming down.

Me: No, it's okay. You need to focus on today. You have that scene with Brooke and you can't be late. Plus, I'm all yucky germs.

Three minutes.

Me: Eli?

One minute.

And then, a knock.

Shit.

My heart swells and sinks and shimmies in the pit of my stomach.

Pulling myself from the warm recesses of my marshmallow cloud mattress, I stumble to the door, knowing my face is splotchy, my eyes swollen, and I look like the most undesirable woman on the island. Still, I pull the door open and almost laugh when Eli gasps.

Gasps.

He steps inside immediately, his right hand going to my forehead, his opposite arm circling my waist. "Zoe, you're burning up."

Is that why I feel so crappy? I can't just deal with the worry of knowing I have cancer, but I also have to spike a fever?

Closing my eyes to stem the emotions already welling inside of me, I lean into Eli's touch. "I don't want to get you sick."

"Fuck that, Violet. What do you need?"

"Sleep."

"A doctor."

"Fine. Sleep and then a doctor."

"Damn it." Grumbling, Eli walks me back toward my bed and tucks me in like a small child, pulling the comforter right up to my chin and fluffing the pillows.

The gesture reminds me of my mom and I grin. "You're going to be the best dad." The words pop from my mouth unexpectedly. Even though my smile doesn't waver, my stomach twists painfully. He *is* going to be the best dad, but his future will have nothing to do with mine.

Eli's tapping out a message on his phone. He fiddles around my room, placing a bottle of water on my nightstand along with my laptop and Kindle. He adds a clean hoodie and fuzzy socks to the end of my bed. When his phone beeps, he finally glances up. "You have an appointment at 4pm. Harlow can take you."

"I'm really fi—"

"Don't say your fine." His eyes harden. I hate the flare of concern that flickers in their depths. "I should have realized sooner; made you see a doctor. Jesus, you've been dealing with these cold symptoms for a whole week."

"Since the morning on your kitchen counter." I smile at the memory.

"Baby, please. Just take care of yourself. Consider our workouts for the week cancelled."

"What? No way." I bolt up in bed, my arms reaching out for him.

He moves to my side and sits next to me, his fingers toying with the ends of my bird's nest hair. "You need rest. And I can't even properly take care of you. So please, just let me do what I can to make sure you get better."

His words plummet into my stomach, like a kick into reality. He thinks he can fix me. Make me better. Help me.

This is just the beginning.

Of what?

The end.

The words fade into my consciousness with a deliberateness that scares me, and I flinch.

Eli sighs, pulling the blankets around my shoulders, thinking it was a chill. "I'm sorry I can't stay with you."

"I'm fine. Go. Report back with all the gossip," I tack on to keep up appearances. I'm not freaking the fuck out.

I'm not.

He smiles, pressing two Advil into my palm. "Take these and close your eyes. If you need anything at all, Harlow is around all day."

"Thank you, Eli."

"Feel better, my Violet."

Once he leaves, I toss back the pills and down some water. Nerves and thoughts and too many feelings to decipher ping-pong through my mind and body, bringing me closer to exhaustion.

When sleep finally claims me, I float away gratefully.

I WAKE up to the sweetest message of my life.

Eli: How are you doing, babe? Thinking of you. X

He sent me a kiss. A kiss that would have made me light up like a Christmas tree three days ago. Today, though, it causes anxiety to swell in my throat like a balloon.

Dr. Salinas and her office were incredibly understanding when they called me back after my nap. In fact, they helped me secure an appointment with a specialist in Victoria for this afternoon.

I send a quick message to Harlow, letting her know I won't need to see the doctor Eli arranged as my own doctor came through. I spend another five minutes convincing her I don't need her to come with me.

Pacing around my room, I glance at the time again and triple-check that my new insurance card, the one with all the medical coverage, is tucked into my wallet.

Another thing Eli has done for me.

My body temperature swings wildly from hot to cold, shivers working up and down my spine. My throat is scratchy, my head throbs, and everything aches.

Finally, it's time. Relieved to be seeing a doctor, I drop my wallet into my purse and leave my hotel room.

The drive to the doctor's office is short. The taxi driver — a humorous man who recently became a grandfather — distracts me for most of the trip with entertaining stories about his first grandson. I nod and smile but my mind is foggy — too many thoughts traveling in too many directions.

When we pull up to the office, a small blue house with a neat white sign out front, he turns in his seat and looks at me, his eyes deep with compassion.

I bite my tongue hard, until the taste of rust fills my mouth.

It's already happening. The pity. The concern. And from a stranger no less. It will be worse when the people I love wear the same expression, only theirs will be laced with hurt from my lies.

"Can I wait for you?"

I shake my head. "No, thank you. I'm not sure how long I'll be."

He nods, passing me a slip of paper with a number scrawled across.

"Taxis are scarce in this part of town. If you need a ride, no matter the time, call me."

"I will. Thank you…"

"Peter."

"Peter." I offer him a smile. I pay the fare, slip from the cab, and walk through the door of the little blue house.

"What did the doctor say?" Charlie's blue eyes blaze with concern as she chomps on the ends of her hair. I know she's trying to keep it together, but her voice cracks and my heart drops.

"That I should have been going for regular screenings."

"And?"

"They won't have the results for several days."

"But they saw something?"

I shrug, looking away as my eyes fill with tears.

"Zoe Claire. What did they see?" My best friend demands an answer, knowing that I'm not being entirely honest.

"I don't know. But the doctor, she says the lump feels

irregular. She doesn't want to say anything until the imaging comes back, but it's probably —"

"No."

"Charlie. I always knew this is —"

"No." Charlie cuts me off again, glaring at me. "You don't know anything yet. Nothing worth panicking over."

I try to swallow past the lump in my throat, but a strangled sound erupts instead. On screen, Charlie winces and her first tears fall.

"Don't you dare cry." I point at her, my tone accusing.

"I can come to you."

"No, you can't," I snort, the idea of Charlie blowing a month's worth of tips on a flight is almost more absurd than me having breast cancer.

"I can." She nods seriously, the damp ends of her ponytail sticking to her neck.

"Charlie, I don't know what to do."

"You're already doing it, Zo. You're living your life."

"I need to call my dad."

Charlie sighs, sucking her lower lip into her mouth. "You do."

"Will you, I don't know, check on him?"

"I'll bring him tea tomorrow morning," my best friend promises. Ducking her head, she swipes the back of her hand across her eyes. "You should tell Eli."

"No."

"Then come home."

"What? Are you serious?" My mouth drops open. "You're the one who's been telling me to live my life."

"You have no support system there, and you're refusing to build one."

"I don't know anything yet," I snap back, arguing her

point from moments earlier. How the hell has this conversation grown so confusing?

"I know. I'm sorry. I'm just...God, I'm worried about you. And I miss you." Charlie forces a smile, her voice breaking.

"I know." I feel my anger melt away as quickly as it soared. Deep down, I know Charlie is just reacting to my news. She's scared for me, like any best friend would be.

"And the cold symptoms? Are they related?"

"No. I actually have an ear and throat infection. I'm relieved the antibiotics are already kicking in because I feel better than I did this morning."

"Well, that's good."

A knock sounds on my door and we both freeze. "Eli."

Charlie swears, shooing at me. "Go. Call me later. After you talk to your dad. I love you."

"Okay. Love you. 'Bye." Disconnecting our call, I close my laptop.

Squaring my shoulders, I wince as Eli knocks again.

"Zoe? Are you okay?" Genuine concern laces his tone.

My heart squeezes painfully in my chest. He's worried about me. And he doesn't even know the worst of it.

I dash my knuckles over my eyes and fluff my hair at the roots.

Glancing at myself in the mirror, I blanch. I look awful.

"Zoe, please. Open up." Eli smacks his palm next to the doorframe.

I pull the door wide open, look up into the most gorgeous face in the world, and allow myself a long moment of drowning in eyes that care about me for all the wrong reasons. "Eli, I'm sorry."

"Hey." He frowns, his brow furrowing as he steps into my

room. The door closes behind him, and I jump from the noise. Eli's frown deepens. He cups my cheek, his thumb swiping once over my cheekbone. "Are you okay? Why haven't you answered my texts?" He looks me over as if expecting to find an injury, blood gushing from some gnarly cut, somewhere on my body.

"Sorry, really. I just, time got away from me." I offer a smile that I know he sees through because he doesn't smile back.

Instead, Eli tilts my head to the side. His eyes rake over my face with precision, doubt coloring his irises. He knows I'm lying, but he doesn't want to call me on it.

He doesn't want to believe I'm deceitful.

"What's going on, Zo? Harlow says you cancelled on the doctor."

I nod, running my palms up his arms until they rest on his shoulders. "I spoke to my doctor. Turned out she has a colleague here."

"And?"

"And, I have an ear and throat infection. I'm taking antibiotics."

Eli's body sags, relief flooding his features. He grips me hard, pulling me flush against his body. "Thank God. I mean, I figured, but I don't know. When you didn't answer my messages, I started to worry that something was really wrong."

"I'm sorry," I murmur against his chest, breathing him in, letting his comfort soothe me even though I don't deserve it. Don't deserve him.

"Don't be sorry. I just want you to feel better."

"I am," I lie, wrapping my arms around him. "Want to grab dinner?"

He glances down, kissing the tip of my nose. "You're hungry?"

I nod.

"Great, yeah. Let's go up to my room and get some room service. I miss sleeping next to you."

"I missed you too." I admit, lacing my fingers with his.

As we walk down the hallway toward the elevator, I feel Eli studying me out of the corner of his eye. He still has a million unasked questions, reservations, and concerns.

All of which will continue to go unanswered.

24

ELI

"You're being weird."

Zoe looks up, the fog clearing from her eyes as she zeroes in on my face, only inches from hers. "No, I'm not."

"You are."

"Am not."

Sighing, I pull her body over mine, letting our legs tangle together. We woke up fifteen minutes ago and while Zoe's been trying to pull me from bed to workout, I'm trying to convince her to rest. Except she's not resting. Not really.

Her mind is going a million miles a minute. Thinking, analyzing, debating.

I have no idea what the hell has her in such a tailspin.

"You going to tell me what's really going on?" I try again, ignoring the edge of panic that's grown with each passing day. Yeah, I know my girl's been sick. But it's more than that. She's putting distance between us, pulling away, so slowly a less broken man wouldn't notice it.

I've been burned before. And I know all the signs.

The excuses. The faraway glances. The lies.

Right now, Zoe's giving me all three.

Zoe rolls her eyes, offering a cheeky grin. Her skin is still sallow, her eyes tired. "I had an ear infection, Holt. And now I need my client to get his ass in gear so I can do my job."

"Back to Holt now?" I question, hating how insecure I feel when two weeks ago, I was barreling through the walls I built to protect myself, too desperate to reach Violet than to care about how she could hurt me.

"Hey." Her hand squeezes mine. "I'm kidding. Why are you taking everything so seriously?" She slips from bed, tugging on a sports bra and leggings.

"Because I thought we were."

She frowns, the tiniest line appearing between her eyebrows. I want to reach out and run my thumb over her smooth skin, iron out the wrinkle.

"Becoming more serious," I clarify.

"We are." She averts her gaze.

"Then tell me what the fuck is going on," I demand, losing my patience as all the thoughts I've been fighting off surge forward. "Is it another guy? Is it too much too soon? Do you hate working with me? Have we blurred too many lines? What is going on? It's more than you just having an ear infection. Be honest with me."

"I am being honest with you. I was sick. I'm sorry if I wasn't myself for a week. You know, I am allowed to get sick, to have an off day, to have a life outside of you." She glares at me, throwing her hands in the air. Anger causes her cheeks to pink and it's such a relief to see her show some goddamn emotion besides dejection that a swirl of relief runs through me.

"Talk to me, Zo. Please." I stand from bed, grabbing workout clothes since Zoe seems hell-bent on sticking to the schedule.

"Just because you shared your life's story with me doesn't

mean I'm obligated to tell you everything," she snaps, swiping a pair of socks off my dresser. "We just started dating, Eli. I mean, is that even what we're doing? No one knows about us. I'm like some dirty little secret you —"

"Is that what this is about? You want to go public? Because I'll walk out of this hotel right now and announce to the entire production that you're my girl." I slap a palm against my bare chest, and Zoe flinches.

She falters, panic edging out her anger.

"Oh, so that's not it?" I cock my head to the side, studying her as I tug on a pair of shorts.

The way her fingers grip the hem of the tank she slipped on, how her hair is tangled around her shoulders, her wide eyes, honey mixed with amber, they're all begging me to — what?

"Last chance, Violet. What's happening here?" I press, my hands curling into fists.

"I'm here to do a job, Hollywood. Stop questioning me on everything and let's get going." She blows me off, walking out of my bedroom. A minute later I hear the chime of the elevator ding.

"Motherfucker," I roar to no one, pulling on a T-shirt. What the hell is going on? I think about skipping the workout, but that's just stupid. I know Zoe is going to do it anyway and I might as well get a sweat in.

For starters, it's part of my job. Yeah, remember that, asshole? The role of a lifetime? The one that's going to change your career.

Except, instead of focusing on it like it's my goddamn priority, I'm losing sleep over a girl I've known for a few months.

But she's *my* girl.

Pinching the bridge of my nose, I swear again. Lacing up

my sneakers, I head toward the beach. If nothing else, maybe a workout will cool both of our tempers enough for a logical conversation.

The thought makes me chuckle. Deep down, I know there's nothing logical about Zoe and me.

And that this is just the beginning.

"Again!"

Sweat rolls down my forehead, stinging my eyes as I narrow my focus on Zoe. She's breathing heavily, her cheeks blazing red, her ponytail sticking to her neck.

Her tank top clings to her skin below her heaving breasts and in the small of her back.

"I said 'again', Holt." Her voice cracks like a whip and I resume my position to start the circuit again. "Faster this time." She manages to spit out before shouting, "Go!"

Swiping my forearm along my face, I start the double jump on the bosu ball before dropping into a burpee with a push-up. Zoe's circuit is tough today, but not enough for her to be lagging the way she is.

Cutting her a quick glance, I take in the sheen of sweat coating her skin. It's more than just exercise sweat. She looks pale, borderline sick. Overwhelmed and completely stressed out.

She is sick, dumb ass. She's still taking antibiotics. She shouldn't be pushing herself like this.

"Keep moving," she mutters.

I'm not sure if she's speaking to me or herself. She swears as the toe of her sneaker catches on the bosu ball and she stumbles. Automatically, I reach out to steady her but she shakes me off, dropping into a push-up.

Why is she so hell-bent on working out today? Why won't she just talk to me?

"You got this," she says again, more quietly this time. Her breathing is labored, her eyes unfocused.

When the timer rings, she resets the clock and turns to me, hands on hips. "Okay. Next up, we're going to run suicide sprints before we jump into weights."

"Violet, wait." I hold out my hand. "I think you need a break. You shouldn't be pushing yourself like this."

"I'm fine. Let's go." She tips her chin toward the next station where she marked out the distance with cones.

Suicide sprints in the sand are no joke. Judging by Zoe's inability to catch her breath, I know she's not up for them.

"Did something happen?" I try again, grateful my concern is still overshadowing the anger building in my veins with every flippant response she tosses my way.

She frowns, her body tensing. Frustration rolls off her shoulders as she scoffs, "No. We're here to work, Holt. So let's get to it."

"Cut the 'Holt' shit for a second and be real with me. You're giving me fucking whiplash. Last week, you were talking about me being your boyfriend, and now you're acting like I'm some kind of disease you have to put up with."

Zoe flinches, stepping back, her hands going to the back of her head. Her skin is flushed, her movements jittery. "I, you..." she pauses, pointing to the first orange marker. "You hired me to do a job, and I'm trying to do it to the best of my ability. Just because we fuck on the side doesn't mean we should slack off. Not me or you."

I rear back as if she physically struck me. Her tone is hard, but her eyes are harder. Darker. Amber like whiskey and just as potent.

Anger beads in my bloodstream, exploding from my mouth in a string of swears. "Fuck on the side? Is that what you're calling it now?" I step toward Zoe, trying to get a read on her emotions.

She shrugs, not backing down, not even dropping her gaze to the sand. "It is what it is."

"Where is this coming from?" I demand, at a complete loss for the sudden one-eighty in her behavior. "It's like everything was great one day and the next, you woke up with a completely different outlook, and I don't know what happened."

Which means, for once, I didn't cause it. I don't think…

"I'm just trying to reassert the boundaries we agreed on."

"What boundaries?"

"You know, you fuck me while we're in the Seychelles and we maintain our professional relationship."

"Yeah, until we discussed making our relationship an actual relationship."

"I can't do that anymore."

"What? Why?"

"I just can't, Holt. I need us to go back to being professional."

"There's absolutely nothing professional about our relationship, and you know it. We blurred that line over two months ago. So what is it? The five-star life not to your liking?" I snap as my temper takes over. Waving my arm wide to encompass the hotel and beach we're standing on, I glare at Zoe, demanding a response.

Zoe's eyes narrow into thin slits, heat crawling up her neck and fanning out across her cheeks.

I swallow back the harsh words on the tip of my tongue, relieved to see her reacting.

Her hands are nearly shaking with fury. "Screw you, Holt."

"Are you on your period or some shit?"

Zoe seethes, her hands clenching into fists, her jawline locking down.

Come on baby, give me something to work with here.

I glare at her, waiting for her to give me an in. A lie I can rip wide open and crawl into with her. Something to fight for, even if it's just our own delusions.

Infuriatingly, she remains tight-lipped, her knuckles turning white.

"Fuck this." I mutter, turning around.

"Hey. We're not done yet," she yells at my back.

Spinning around, I chuckle humorlessly. "Aren't we, though?"

"Get back here, Holt. We have three more circuits."

"Take the rest of the day, Zoe." I wave without turning around and walk back to the hotel, adrenaline coursing through my veins like a damn drug.

I knew this casual, easygoing, live-in-the-moment shit was too good to be true. She flipped her switch like all women end up doing, blindsiding me. And for what? What crawled up her ass and died?

That's the million-dollar question.

Storming into a side door, I nearly collide with Harlow. "Damn, are you okay?" I reach out to steady her.

"Are you?"

"Fine."

"You sound like a woman."

"Leave it alone, Harlow." I storm toward the elevators and sigh when she steps in after me.

The ride to my suite is silent. When the elevator doors ding open, I stalk into the penthouse, slamming my fist on the kitchen island before moving to the living room. Hopped up on adrenaline and anger, I have no idea what the hell to do with myself.

Harlow passes me a beer from the refrigerator. "Here."

Dropping to the couch, I mumble thanks and close my eyes. My fist clenches the bottle, and some of the cold seeps into my skin, cooling my temper.

I feel the couch dip next to me. I turn to glance at my assistant-turned-friend-turned family. "Zoe's shutting me out."

"Me too." Harlow murmurs. I can tell she's hurt.

"Did something happen?"

She shrugs. "Not that I know of."

"I mentioned giving our thing a real go. Like a relationship."

Harlow's eyes widen as she stares at me. "That's huge for you."

"I know."

"What happened?"

"Zoe seemed all for it. Then she got sick, this ear infection bullshit, and totally flipped the script."

"She's not really talking to me either. I mean, she is, but it's too polite, too formal."

"Yeah." I take a swig of my beer. "She's suddenly throwing boundaries and a professional relationship in my face."

"Hmm."

I snap my neck back toward Harlow. "What the hell does 'hmm' mean?"

"She's a smart girl, Eli."

"Meaning?"

"You draw lines in the sand all day long. They crisscross each other, intersecting in random patterns, and it's all okay as long as it works for you. For everyone else, though, they're arbitrary. Seems to me Zoe's doing the same thing, and you don't like it. She's protecting herself."

"From what?"

"Isn't it obvious? You."

"That's ridiculous. I'd never hurt her."

"Not intentionally, no. Or maybe I have it wrong," she says slowly, tapping her fingertips against her mouth.

"What?"

"Maybe it's the other way around. Maybe she doesn't want to hurt *you*."

I stare at Harlow for a long beat, the stretch of silence hanging between us like a thread. Then, I burst out laughing, snap the thread, and shake my head. "You're the fucking best, Low."

"I'm not kidding, Eli."

"Yeah. Okay. How the hell could Violet hurt me?"

"You like her too much."

"I don't like anyone enough to hurt me anymore."

"Then why are you drinking beer, silently fuming?"

Sobering, I clamp my mouth shut and stare back at the ceiling. "I hate it when you make sense."

Harlow's smile doesn't reach her eyes. "So do I."

We sit on the couch for a long time, watching the shadows on the wall shrink. Finally, she pulls herself up and shoots me a sympathetic look. "Just have a quiet night. Give her space, and don't do anything stupid."

"Like what?"

"Like stupid. Just hang in tonight and chill. Talk to her tomorrow." She gives me one more knowing glance over her shoulder before slipping out of the penthouse.

Yeah right. Haven't I already messed up enough for one

day? As much as I appreciate Harlow's advice, even I know I should call Violet. Check on her.

Her behavior today was so out of character. I shouldn't have pushed her the way I did. Maybe she needs someone to be there for her, and I pushed her away when I should have pulled her closer. Haven't I learned anything from Natalie? The entire time she was lashing out, it was because she was desperate for someone to care enough to rein her in.

Closing my eyes, I fall in and out of sleep until the chime of my phone wakes me several hours later.

I pick it up, certain it's Zoe.

Instead, my stomach drops and I bolt to my feet, knocking over the bottle of beer.

Natalie: Hey Eli. I just landed in the Seychelles. Please, can we talk? Just hear me out…

25

ZOE

The moon casts a pale glow on the ocean as I wade into the gently lapping waves. The water, a vibrant green in daylight, is darker now. Inviting in its depth, comforting in its calmness. The hairs on my arms stand on end as a chill rolls down my spine, but the coldness is emanating from within, causing my blood to slow with chips of ice.

I'm numb. So numb that my pounding heart and dry eyes don't register. I see only the moonlight, the way it glances off the tops of cresting waves. I feel only sand rising between my toes with each step. I sense only the caress of the sea as it swallows me, inching up my thighs, my bare belly, covering my breasts and the threatening secrets they contain.

I breathe in the salt and hold it in my lungs as I drag my body under water, exploding up into the air and shrieking. My hair, still thick and full, sticks to the tops of my back in wet clumps. A childlike freeness surrounds me and I laugh, running my fingertips through the water, floating on its gentleness.

Alone, with only the sea turtles and seashells to keep me company.

It's liberating in a strange sense. My chest swells once more with the strength I'll undoubtedly need in the long months ahead.

The sky is inky, swatches of darkness illuminated by single pinpricks of light. I lie on my back, floating aimlessly, letting the water fill my ears and lap over the top of my body. My breath enters and exits my lungs on tiny wisps, an echo I can hear below the waterline.

My body flushes hot and cold. My eyes sting and burn.

A shooting star arcs across the night sky and I gasp, my fingers pressing into my lips.

Did anyone see it but me?

The sea wraps around me like a hug, comforting and calming. My body shivers, my fingers trembling against my face.

I pushed him away.

Eli. I was callous and hurtful to force space between us. To make him leave before he has to.

God, what did I do?

For over two months, I encouraged him to drink my lies straight from my lips while I collected his truths like tiny pebbles. I saved them in the hallow of my belly until they swelled large enough to choke me, stamping out my ability to breathe freely, to think clearly. I let him carve a place inside of me that belongs to only him.

I knew better.

My hands clench, gripping at the sea even as the water seeps through my fingers.

Like Eli, I never should have tried to hold on to something so fleeting.

It's better this way. I mouth the words to the moon, but no sound comes out.

His face, contorted in rage, flickers through my mind.

His eyes, oh. Bright and bleeding. Begging and open.

He trusted me. And I hurt him.

Maybe not as deeply as Natalie but hurt is still pain. What's the use in arguing over its source to the one drowning in it?

I hold my breath and dip my head, letting the sea wash over my face. The moon grows hazy in my vision as my eyes burn from the salt.

A million pinpricks of light. Stars. Wishes.

You love him.

I love him.

I break the surface of the water, the realization slamming into me with so much force, I inhale the sea and sputter.

I pushed Eli away because I'm in love with him. Not just falling. Not just enjoying the moment. But so fucking in love with him that if I close my eyes, I can see the future he wants. The one with the house and the basketball team of kids that I'll never give him. Too scared to admit that, I pretended I didn't want it.

Didn't want him.

But I do. Oh God, I want it all so badly it aches and breaks my heart to know I'll never have it.

Eli should know the truth. He should know how I feel.

After all, didn't I want this incredible bit of the human experience? To fall in love. To know what the entire point of living really is. And now, I have it, and I'm too scared to admit it.

I want to own my truth.

Shaking my head at the moon, I grin and say a silent thank you to the stars. I scramble to the shoreline, wrapping my naked body in a towel I swipe from a lounge chair. Then I pick up my wallet and phone from the sand and start for the hotel.

I need to get dressed.

No. I need to find Eli.

I slip into one of the robes folded neatly on the sun loungers next to the pool and jab my hands through the arm holes until I can pull it on. Tugging my hair out the neck, I grip the front of the robe tightly, slip my wallet and phone into the pocket, and beeline for the elevator.

I don't want to feed Eli any more lies. I want him to know my truth. The feelings of my heart. The secrets of my soul. The truth about *us*.

Fishing his key card out of my wallet, I press P for Penthouse.

My nerves rattle around the entire elevator ride up.

I hope he's happy to see me. I hope he kisses me senseless and makes love to me right on the marble floor of the foyer.

Moments later, the door opens and I step out into —

"Eli?" His name dies on my lips as I nearly collide with his frame.

He's shirtless, the muscles of his chest and shoulders tense with disbelief. Sweats hang low on his hips, the drawstring sticking out of his pants as if he tugged them on in a hurry. The stubble on his cheeks is more pronounced, his neck straining, his jawline sharp enough to crack cement. But his eyes stare at me with so much hurt and betrayal that I feel fissures form in my chest, little pieces of my heart disintegrating with guilt. I open my mouth but before I can form any words, my eyes land on the other figure in the room.

Twisting my neck, my eyes lock onto Natalie Beck's. I gasp, my knees going weak as I try to make sense of the scene unfolding in front of me.

"What the fuck are you doing here?" Eli nearly roars.

I flinch, unprepared for the malice in his tone, unsure if he's speaking to me or to her.

"Eli." Her voice bleeds with urgency. "Please, just let me explain."

"No," he cuts her off, his gaze swinging back to mine.

Fear, confusion, betrayal. The green depths of his eyes swirl, violent and turbulent.

I open my mouth again, but before my truth can tumble out, Natalie speaks. "Eli, I'm pregnant."

Eli and Zoe's emotional and captivating love story continues in *Twisted Truths*. Read Now!

TWISTED TRUTHS

Eli Holt swallows the lies I feed him and exhales them as twisted truths.

He believes in our future; he believes in us.

At least he did until I force him to hate me.

Witnessing Eli retreat into himself, erecting walls too high for me to scale cuts me to my core.

I lie to protect his future but I never anticipate Eli discovering my secret, learning my truth.

The moment he does, he embraces my anguish, his love healing all the dark parts of my soul.

Relentless. Determined. Desperate.

I couldn't push Eli away again if I tried, even if keeping him destroys us both.

Read Now!

ALSO BY GINA AZZI

The Kane Brothers Series:
Rescuing Broken (Jax's Story)
Recovering Beauty (Carter's Story)
Reclaiming Brave (Denver's Story)
My Christmas Wish
(A Kane Family Christmas
+ *One Last Chance* FREE prequel)

Finding Love in Scotland Series:
My Christmas Wish
(A Kane Family Christmas
+ *One Last Chance* FREE prequel)
One Last Chance (Daisy and Finn)
This Time Around (Aaron and Everly)

The College Pact Series:
The Last First Game (Lila's Story)
Kiss Me Goodnight in Rome (Mia's Story)
All the While (Maura's Story)
Me + You (Emma's Story)

Standalone
Corner of Ocean and Bay

ACKNOWLEDGMENTS

Writing the Second Chance Chicago series was a true labor of love. I've never felt so connected to characters before or invested in their relationships - romantic, platonic, familial - as I have in these books! *Broken Lies* challenged me and pushed me out of my comfort zone, and yet, I loved every second of exploring Zoe and Eli's love story and getting to know the characters who support them.

To Becca Mysoor - Thank you for all the incredible feedback and honest conversations!! The finished product of this duet would be nowhere near where it is without your guidance. YOU'RE THE BEST!

To Regina Wamba - I am loving your photoshop classes!! Thank you for giving me the confidence and providing the tools to allow me to create my own covers for this duet.

To Amelia Wilde - who stepped in at the eleventh hour and helped me with all things book covers. You're amazing!

To MPP - I'd certainly lose the plot without you. Thanks for all of your support but more than that, for your friendship. Ocean girls for life!

To JA Owenby - I love all our book chats and appreciate

all of your help leading up to the launch of *Broken Lies*! So happy we connected!

To all the bloggers, bookstagrammars, and readers - THANK YOU! Your support means everything and I truly appreciate your taking a chance on me. I hope you adore this story as much as I do.

All the thanks to my family! To my dad, for talking through plot points and brainstorming outrageous scenarios. To my mom, for listening when I get stuck. To my brother, for chatting all things logistics. I wouldn't dare chase my dreams if it wasn't for you.

And, of course, my Home Team - Tony, Aiva, Rome, Luna - you are the best part of this adventure! Love you with all my heart.

Get ready for Twisted Truths!

XO,

Gina

ABOUT THE AUTHOR

Gina Azzi writes emotional and captivating contemporary romance novels with heart-warming happily-ever-afters. She is the author of *Second Chance Chicago Series*, *The Kane Brothers Series*, *The College Pact Series*, *Finding Love in Scotland Series*, and *Corner of Ocean and Bay*.

A Jersey girl at heart, Gina has spent her twenties traveling the world, living and working abroad, before settling down in Ontario, Canada with her husband and three children. She's a voracious reader, daydreamer, and coffee enthusiast who loves meeting new people. Say hey to her on social media or through www.ginaazzi.com.

Made in the USA
Middletown, DE
25 April 2023